MW01241498

The Endless Seasons of Love

R. Lataine Townsend

Copyright & ISBN Page

Copyrighted ©1996, revised version deposited 2014
R. Lataine Townsend
All rights reserved.

ISBN 13: 9781493601387
ISBN: 1493601385

Library of Congress Control Number: 2013921895
CreateSpace Independent Publishing Platform
North Charleston, South Carolina

For Paul Mueller
April 8, 1933 – December 28, 1990

Without his help
I could never have come this far.

His favorite quote:
"Daily everything lay in God's hands trusting."

"The autumn crocus always harkened the coming of winter."

Cover photo from dreamstime.com
Photo above by the author

Part One

Part Two

Part One

Chapter 1

Late Summer

The little cart wound its way across the valleys of farms and through forests of oak and chestnut. The journey from *Saint-Léonard de Noblat* had been four days and the climb became steeper as they neared the *Mássif*. The cart slowed and the little donkey seemed to struggle a bit.

"He is old like me," apologized the old man with a fleeting smile.

"Stop the cart," the nun said softly. "I will walk with him again," she said as she jumped agilely from the cart. She patted the little one and encouraged him with 'cluckings' as she began to walk. "Come," she said softly and the animal followed more smoothly. The road became steeper. She noticed the scent of the trees and the coolness of their shade. She was glad to be reaching her new home before nightfall. The sun was near setting as they turned a bend and the church came into view on a rise to the left of the road. A low stone wall surrounded the entire collection of buildings. The church, built of the large grey stones of the area, had a simple beauty. The *dormitorie* of the same stone was attached to the right side of the chapel and beyond it there seemed to be a stable and gardens. The area of graves was on the other side of the chapel on lower ground.

The cart rattled onto the cobblestone cloister and ceased its noise as she halted the donkey. As the old man climbed down slowly and made the reins fast on the hook, a priest and a plump matronly nun appeared from the side door.

"*Pace e bene*, welcome," the priest said smiling. "I am Father Paolo and this is Mother Marguerite. You are Sister Janine."

She noted his quote of St. Francis before she replied with head bowed, "I am." As she looked up, her eyes briefly met his of clearest blue, which surprised her since she had already noticed his hair was dark. Her eyes dropped quickly as she felt a soft flutter inside.

"I see you walk with the little one," the priest said.

"Yes, the way becomes difficult here, but God's creation is so beautiful here," she replied.

"Yes, yes, it is . . . everywhere," he said, glancing at her then lifting his eyes to the valleys and hills. "Will you take evening repast and lodgings with us, *Monsieur*?" he inquired of the old man.

"No. Thank you, Father. I have a brother in the village next and will take back cheeses to Limoges after a pilgrimage to *Conques*."

"Ah, yes, *Conques*. Little St. Foy, beheaded and burned and no one knows how the child displeased the Emperor Diocletian," responded Father Paolo sadly.

The old man turned to his cart. "I have plates for the merchant in the village and the maker has sent one for your blessed service," he said, carefully handing the priest a plate wrapped in cloth.

"Thank you, may you be blessed," said Father Paolo, indicating that he knew the gift was actually from the old man, "and may the craftsman be blessed in his skill."

"Thank you, *Monsieur*," Sister Janine said as the old man handed the small bag to her. "Your travels will be easier on the road back down," she said, glancing tenderly at the little donkey and smiling.

The cart clattered out of the compound as Janine turned to follow the priest and the Mother Superior. She noticed the sunset seemed to be turning everything to gold, reminding her of quotes referring to heaven. Father Paolo went through a side entrance into the chapel and Sister Marguerite said, "I will show you to your cell, Sister. Sister Jacqueline and Sister Clare are in the chapel and will welcome you at supper. There is a well through this door," she indicated as she led her to the back of the refectory. "You may wish to refresh yourself," she added, glancing at her dusty hem. As the Mother Superior led the way up the steep narrow steps, Janine noticed there were four doorways as they proceeded to the farthest one. "This room will be cold in winter, but it is very nice in spring and fall. Evening meal is at eight bells until the equinox. Father Paolo's schedule may be a bit different from what you were used to at the orphanage convent," she added, eyebrows slightly raised. "Welcome," she said warmly as she quietly closed the door behind her.

Janine looked around the small room. The cot appeared to be fluffy with fresh straw, and there were two wool blankets. The little table had a full pitcher and a bowl, towel and cloth. The wall above the bed had a single crucifix and the little window looked out over gardens, meadows and trees. Above those, she could see the distant hills. Her heart was full of thankfulness as she knelt beside her wooden cot.

Chapter 2

Early Fall

Sister Janine had scarcely seen Father Paolo except at mass. He seemed to be always busy with keeping the church self-supportive and "tending his flock." He had taken most of his meals in his room near the bell tower, which she understood was unusual from a few comments by the sisters. Yes, the schedule was different from the convent in *Sainte Leonard* where she had worked in the orphanage. When she had heard of the need for help with teaching the children of this parish near *Villefranche*, Janine had volunteered.

Father Paolo was a firm believer in the Franciscan rule of self-sufficiency and humility and Mother Marguerite seemed to be in full accord. She had to wonder how they accomplished everything before she came. She now carried the wood to the kitchen before matins and after prayers, brought water from the spring-fed well. Sister Jacqueline was responsible for the morning meal and Janine thought her talents must lie elsewhere. Cleaning the kitchen and refectory and mopping the stone floors of the nave were the chores Janine had to finish before mass. Sister Clare was scarcely able to walk, so stiff were her joints; she kept at her weaving between prayers and offices. A cell had been made for her in a pantry area by the kitchen since she could no longer climb the stairs. The soft beige habits they all wore were Clare's handiwork and many of the poorer parishioners were recipients of her cloth as well. Most in the parish were poor, very poor. Wars of one kind or another had ravaged across the area for so many generations, the people seemed never to recover. When there was no war, there was plague or other sickness.

Upon learning that Sister Janine was knowledgeable about many herbs, Father Paolo had asked Mother Marguerite to have her spend any spare time between *sext* and vespers walking in the meadows and forest searching for wood sorrel, coltsfoot, althea roots and any other herbs she thought might be beneficial.

"Sister Janine, I will pray for your safety, but be very watchful," Mother Marguerite had said.

Janine had heard the rumors of the crimes directed against the Church in areas of the Languedoc. Those called Huguenots were striking back after the Church had tried to stamp out this new heresy that had arisen. The massacre in the area of the *Vaudois* had shocked everyone. That area from *Albi* to the Pyrenees Mountains had been in turmoil it seemed for centuries. The Cathar heresy had led to the barons taking up a crusade of blood against the Provence. She never had understood the conflict, for the Cathari believed in extreme asceticism almost like the Friars Minor. But the Dominican friars had helped in many instances to hunt down the heretics and burn them. There were many things she did not understand, she thought to herself, as she walked. The flowers of summer were gone but the meadows were still beautiful as they began to take on the gold tones of autumn.

"I have found cress and greens for the supper pie," Janine told Sister Jacqueline when she returned from the meadow, and placed the freshly washed leaves on the table. "I will dry the other herbs under my cot," she said as she went up the stairs. She carefully placed the leaves and roots in separate groups. The vespers bell was ringing as she hurriedly brushed off her skirt and sleeves.

"The turnip pie is very good," said Father Paolo at evening repast. "Where did you find the greens?"

"Sister Janine found them as she was walking," Jacqueline replied looking at Janine coldly.

"Yes? And what else did you find, Sister?" he asked, looking up briefly.

"I did find the coltsfoot and a little snakeroot and also some mustard leaf; the gentian does not seem very plentiful here. I did not have time to go far into the woods," she replied.

"Wonderful! These may prove helpful to our flock. Mother Marguerite, please ring the bell for *compline* and turn the hourglass. I will be in the village late. I must talk with two of our own who are in disagreement. Poverty always seems to turn neighbors against each other. How can I convince them to trust in God's love when their families scarcely have enough to eat? Oh yes . . . Sisters, please bar the *dormitorie*; I shall come in through the back door of the chapel." His face carried signs of concern as he left the refectory.

After the kitchen was spotless under Mother Marguerite's watchful eye and Sister Jacqueline had departed to her room, Janine sat down by Sister Clare who was already at her loom.

"Sister Clare, how are your knees today?" asked Janine.

"They are the same, Sister, but now I fear the affliction has come to my hands. How shall I serve if I cannot weave?"

"Oh, Sister Clare," Janine replied, "Your prayers are a great service and you shall always be able to pray. I am searching for the rue and skullcap as well as the gentian root. We will make a tea for you when I find them. That will help."

"You are a great blessing to us, child," Clare said. "I have a little coverlet for your cot, she said as she pulled a length of mutely colored cloth from under her weaving.

"This is beautiful, Sister Clare," Janine said, "But will I be allowed to have it? You know our teaching."

"Mother Marguerite will recognize the source and will allow it," Clare replied with a sly smile. "Now, help me to a seat near the altar and I shall stay in prayer until *compline*."

"I will stay with you," Janine replied softly as she guided her slowly.

Chapter 3

Early Winter

"Sister Janine, go to the side door, a beggar in rags is there. I saw him coming onto the cloister," ordered Sister Jacqueline.

As Janine left the scrubbing tub full of habits and dried her hands, she looked sadly at Jacqueline disappearing toward the chapel.

"Come into the kitchen," she said quietly as she opened the barred door of the *dormitorie*. The man was clad in several layers of ragged clothes and his shoes were in worse condition. His face was smudged with smoke and soot. He edged closer to the fireplace burning at the end of the room. Janine gathered as much bread and roasted chicken as she dared and placed it in a clean towel and tied it. As he thanked her, she recognized but did not fully understand the Aragon dialect.

"May your journey over the mountains be safe," she said for she knew he was probably trying to return home after shepherding in the north all summer. It appeared he had been attacked and his summer's wages had been taken. There were many different stories that came with these frightened ones that stopped by their side door. Father Paolo never sent one on his way without food. She wondered why Jacqueline was so repulsed by them.

She lifted the heavy kettle back onto the hook in the fireplace and went outside to sweep the light snow off the stone cloister.

Her prayers, she felt, could be heard here as well as in the chapel. Father Paolo was attending a diocesan meeting in Lyon and her prayers were for his safe return. She brought in more firewood and resumed her rinsing of the laundry. Mother Marguerite appeared to help her hang it all to dry in the large kitchen.

"Mother Marguerite, how long have you served here?" Janine asked.

"Almost four years," she replied. "Sister Clare and four others were here when Mother Claudine went to God. I came from a convent near *Chartres*; you've probably heard of the beautiful cathedral there. But, there is much unrest among the people there. The price of wheat and flour has almost doubled, the rents on the lands have been raised by almost all landlords, and so many have been put off their land and join the vagabonds that roam and beg and steal. What can we do to help when so many are homeless? Ah . . . I'm sorry, Sister Janine, to ramble on so; sometimes I despair for our people."

"Yes, Mother Marguerite, I have even in my time seen many sad things. The orphanage at St. Leonard had much sadness," Janine replied.

"Were you there as a child, Sister?" Marguerite asked.

"No, I was fortunate to be taken by my aunt and uncle when my parents died in an outbreak of the plague. Our *domus* was burned. It was known that I would enter God's service from that time, so I was prepared most of my life. I was a servant in my uncle's home, but my mother had requested on her deathbed that I be sent to teachers," she explained.

"And, Sister Jacqueline, is she from this district?" Janine asked.

"No, I don't think so, very little is known; she has never spoken of her past. She came from a convent near Dijon and I understood her parents were of nobility, but never has she spoken of them," Marguerite said.

"Has Father Paolo been here very long?" Janine asked.

"No," replied Marguerite smiling, "less than a year, but already he has the hearts of these people. He has been so much help to them, not like our last priest who scarcely bothered to say mass. We depended then entirely on the parish and many of them looked to us for help! Father *Tomás* received many francs from the bishop and abbot. He had three servant girls from the village to do chores and . . . well, it is best not to say what one has not seen." She broke off suddenly and quietly went toward the chapel, head bowed.

Janine had caught her implication. She knew concubinage or *promiscuite'* had been a problem in the clergy for as long as the Rule had been in existence. She wondered what Father Paolo's feelings were on this subject. He seemed to emulate St. Francis in every way - almost. The Saint had avoided looking at women and it was said he forbade his followers to speak to women. But it was also said that St. Francis liked the larks best of all birds because they were dressed like nuns, their heads capped by a small brown hood. And, of course, the Poor Clares were of his founding.

Chapter 4

Late Winter

"The water has boiled?" Janine asked as she peeked out from the side room.

"It is just beginning, Sister," Father Paolo replied. "Can we be of any help?" he asked.

"Only your prayers," she softly replied. "I've done all that can be done." She stepped back into the room and pulled the curtain. She wished for leaves of the *myrra* tree but trusted the wisdom of God in this.

The woman looked very tired and pale. "Will I lose the child?" she asked.

"Yes, Beatrice, I think it is to be," Janine replied. "None of the remedies are slowing the flow."

"Forgive me, Sister, but I feel sad and happy," she said with tears welling up in her eyes. "We cannot provide all the things needed for our two little ones now." She groaned through clenched teeth. Janine took her hand again.

"It is fully like birthing," Beatrice said, squeezing her hand.

"Yes, do not be distressed; God sees our troubles. Breathe deeply. Sip the tea of angelica if you can," Janine directed. She quickly pulled a soft blanket from the bag she had brought and stepped to the end of the bed. With another groan, the woman sighed deeply. Janine quickly checked and found the female child very premature and malformed, incapable of surviving.

"Please wring the cloths and bring them in the bowl that I set there," she asked of Father Paolo.

The woman lay back weakly. Janine quickly cleaned the pitiful little baby and the mother and began to expertly massage the woman's abdomen.

"Father Paolo, please wrap the child in the little blanket and take it; the afterbirth seems slow," Janine requested as he brought the sterile cloths. She did not miss a stroke as she looked up into his eyes and nodded in the negative. He gently wrapped the little body and slipped out quietly.

"Beatrice, the little girl was not old enough to live outside; she has gone back to God," Janine said gently.

Beatrice nodded her head and tears spilled over as she closed her eyes.

"You must stay in bed until I come tomorrow afternoon. Use the night bowl; do not go out to the *latrine*. I am leaving some leaves of raspberry and fruit of rose. Have Raymonde make a tea three or four times a day for as long as it lasts and send for me if you must use more than these cloths that are on the table." Janine quietly removed the soiled linens and put fresh ones under her patient. She knelt beside the low bed, put her arms around the young woman and held her gently.

"You will be fine now. We will talk more tomorrow; rest and regain your strength and allow God's healing to begin," Janine said as she smoothed the woman's hair. Beatrice nodded.

As she slipped through the curtain and began tending the linens, Father Paolo was speaking quietly with Raymonde about the service and burial. When she was finished and had given full instructions to Raymonde, they pulled on their heavy, hooded cloaks and stepped out into the night snowstorm.

"Thank you for coming with me," Father Paolo said. "Though, I worked in the 'Hôpital' in Paris, the villagers seem untrusting, especially where their women are concerned. I think it has to do with incidents with either the previous priest or the physician that was here briefly two or three years ago."

"Yes, there have been words to that effect spoken to me also," Janine replied, remembering what Mother Marguerite had begun to say.

"Well, we shall be judged by our works, Sister; and by the next liturgy the entire village will know of your care tonight. I admire your knowledge of the herbs and roots. Where were you taught this? At the convent?" he asked.

"No," she replied as they began the climb that led up to the church. "My grandmother lived with my aunt who took me when my parents died. She was very knowledgeable and would take me for long walks, even when I was quite young and point out each plant and name each tree and tell me how God placed all things here for our use. I'm not sure when I began to have a sort of 'knowing.' When I placed my hands on a sick one, I had a sense of what the malady was and the thought of a plant would come to me."

"Why did you not use this gift in the *hôpitals*?" he asked incredulously. "And you worked in an orphanage?!"

"Yes . . . well, there was in *Bourganeuf* a woman who had similar gifts and it was said that she could touch and heal. She was . . . ah . . . a little different in . . . her beliefs and there were those who feared her powers. The story is unclear, but she was apparently accused of heresy and impiety and burned outside the walls of the town. I was thirteen at that time and I never spoke of my abilities to anyone after that. I cannot keep from sharing the herbs with those I can help, but I have not allowed the gift free rein; perhaps, I am wrong," she confided.

"No, Sister Janine, in this time there is much evil done in the name of our Lord," he replied, taking her arm as she slipped on the snow. "There are those that use the edicts of our Holy Church and the superstitions of the uneducated to fill their own pockets and gain their own objectives."

Janine had never felt anything like the feelings that were going through her now as he guided her safely up the hill. Her mind was a jumble and she forgot what the conversation was about. They walked in silence. As they reached the cloister, he abruptly asked, "Have you found any of the black willow in your searches?"

She was glad it was dark for her face flushed. Not everyone knew the use of the black willow, but she knew of its use in keeping the passions controlled. "Yes, there is a cluster by the small creek in the forest to the rising sun," she replied. "I will bring some in the spring at the right time."

"Well, it will be time for *matins* bell before we are scarcely asleep; I will not expect you at prayers this bell," he said gently smiling, knowing all the while that she would never miss an office.

"Thank you again," he said opening the door to the *dormitorie* and handing her a candle lighter stick from the fireplace.

"I was happy to help," Sister Janine replied as she went up the stairs quietly. Sister Jacqueline's door closed almost silently as she went past to her own room. As she lit her candle, she noticed the water was frozen in her bowl and pitcher. She laid her cloak over her blankets, but hardly noticed the cold as she drifted off into a restless sleep.

Chapter 5

Early Spring

"Mother Marguerite, the Rule that our Saint Benedict wrote in the year of our Lord 540, maintained that each community in His service should be sufficient in itself," said Father Paolo.

"But, Father Paolo," she replied, "many things have changed, this is not 540. The Rule also required worship, study and prayers. Even the guide of our sainted Francis whom you follow has changed."

"Sister, our people are taxed and oppressed enough; can we also ask them to further give to us when we can give to them?" he asked.

"But, a cow? And chickens? These entail much care and our holy offices must be observed," Marguerite responded. "I am not familiar with these . . . these . . . animals," she sputtered.

"Sister Janine grew up among the shepherds and farming, surely she can help when I am away," Father Paolo said.

"Sister Janine is already overburdened, though she never complains. Father, you do not seem to understand that not all have the vigor that you have. However, we are obedient in your rule and will do our best. Perhaps Sister Janine will be helpful in choosing this . . . this cow," Marguerite said wryly.

Janine's thoughts were still on Sister Jacqueline as they walked through the village toward the market place. Jacqueline had looked at her with such hatred when Father Paul had announced that Janine would do the marketing this week since he wanted her opinion on the selection of the cow. Jacqueline had turned abruptly on her heel and walked toward the chapel.

"This is the *domus* of Claude Benet and his wife, Mary," Father Paolo pointed out as they walked down the hill. "He is a spurrier by trade, but, of course, most of his bits and tack and spurs are taken either to Marseille or Lyon. I understand some have even been requested and sent to Barcelona in the Kingdom of Aragon. There are more horses in those areas." They walked on into the village.

"And, of course, you know Raymonde and Beatrice across the way there. Since the night the baby was stillborn, I have seen many changes there; both are now faithful to mass and confession and I see them working together more and teaching the children gently. Even Chamfor, the *boucher*, remarked about the work Raymonde does with him in the slaughtering. We are very fortunate in such a small village to have such a variety of trades and crafts."

"I see our market even has a *banchi* today, exchanging dracmas and florins for francs," Janine noted. "Our trade is reaching many far places. Have you ever traveled to the Holy City, Father Paolo?" she asked.

"Oh, yes, Sister Janine, and it is so very beautiful. The cathedral at St. Peter's tomb is nearing completion. I have heard it is to have a great dome. A man named Michelangelo is in charge of the building and I have heard that he will accept no monies for his work. He is the same one who painted the beautiful frescoes in the chapel of the Pope's Palace. A remarkable man . . . over seventy years of age. Did you know that it was in the year of my birth that the Spaniards attacked the Holy City and, from May to September, murdered over twelve thousand people? Over half of the dwellings were destroyed. They stabled horses in the blessed Sistine Chapel. The torture and looting were the worst in our times," he said shaking his head sadly. "The high wall and towers built by Pope Leo in 852 did not keep them out. The Saracens had already taken all valuables and violated the tomb of St. Peter. There is a stone altar house now that stands over the shrine. It was Pope Paul who called in Michelangelo to resume the construction that had halted with the great desolation by the mercenaries. It will be the grandest offering in all Christendom. I was there three years ago and saw its magnificence. This Sistine Chapel that I spoke of is also very beautiful with painting by this same Michelangelo on the ceiling. And the library! It is beyond description. I spent many hours there.

"The masses have the music of great organs and choirs . . . it is hard to describe how wonderful the feeling is there," he said, shaking his head. "Have you never traveled, Sister?" he asked.

"No, not widely. My life has been spent between the *Vienne*, *Loire* and the *Lot* Rivers, the central area of the *Valois* kingdoms. I have heard of the great seas, but I have not seen them," Janine replied as they strolled among the various carts of goods.

"You must tell me about Limoges at some time, for I have never been there," *Paolo* requested.

They chose some cheese from one vendor and candles from another. It was so comfortable to be with Father Paolo; Janine wanted to ask many more questions about his past, but held back, not feeling sure that it was proper. They had reached the area where several farmers had brought cows, heifers and even one bull to sell. Father Paolo began talking affably with the villagers that he already knew. Janine trailed along listening and enjoying.

Chapter 6

Spring

"Forgive me, Father, for I have sinned. It has been a week since my last confession. Father, I have again fallen asleep during my evening prayers," Janine intoned softly.

Father Paolo hesitated to speak for so long, Janine almost began again, then he said, "Sister, you have not fallen asleep, you have entered into an ecstasy, such as our revered Saint Francis and others have experienced. I have on rare occasion felt this also. It is not sleep; it is communion with God. You do not wake with sleepfulness as in the morning, but with quick clarity, do you not?"

"Yes, Father," she replied. "I feel as if I am at peace and harmony with all creation."

"There is no sin; there is no penance. It is a great gift; if only all had this . . . 'sin.' Is there something else, my child?" he asked.

"Yes, Father." She hesitated.

"Go on, Sister," he encouraged.

"Even in my dreams I am in conflict with Sister Jacqueline. I dreamed that I was roughly tumbling about with her, fighting her. Forgive me, Father; I try to love all," she said weakly.

"My child, our holy scriptures reads 'a house divided against itself shall not stand.' Is it possible that you are fighting with yourself on some matter and not Sister Jacqueline at all? Look within your heart."

"Yes, Father, there is something unsettled within my heart, but my confession will have to be made elsewhere," she replied, knowing the strong feelings that she had at times toward him and the equally strong commitment to her vows to God.

"Go with the peace of God in your heart," he intoned.

"Thank you, Father," she said softly as she left the confessional.

Paolo sat a long time thinking of his own ambivalence and Janine's sweet nature. She was so trusting and felt others pain so acutely. He wished all the confessions he heard were so unctuous. He rose and went toward the tower to ring the bell for vespers. As he passed the chapel, he noticed Janine had already knelt in prayer behind the chancel. Her beauty at times overwhelmed that barrier he had put up when he had made his decision to serve God. He had known of parishes where priest and nuns lived in 'carnal knowledge.' In some cases, this was even known to the parishioners and accepted. He had chosen to give his energies to God and now these feelings of the flesh were nibbling at that decision.

Chapter 7

Summer

Janine and *Madame de Roquefort* had wandered farther than usual - Madame in search of sweeter clover and she in search of snakeroot and wild garlic. Sister Clare had patiently drank the teas and submitted to the warm poultices on her knees and shoulders, but nothing seemed to reverse the insidious progress of the stiffness. Janine sat down on the grass under a large oak, holding Madame's rope as she grazed nearby. Her thoughts were on Sister Clare; her eyes closed. She jumped when she heard a sound to one side.

"Oh, Father Paolo," she whispered, her hand over her pounding heart, "I did not see you come."

"I'm sorry. It was such a beautiful day I decided to walk to clear my thoughts." He paused and glanced around. "I have been reading some of the writings of John Wycliffe who is at Oxford in England and Meister Eckhart who lived near the Rhine in the Holy Roman Empire. I want to take only the simple teachings of our St. Francis of Assisi, but the world is not the same now. Many are questioning the extent of God's creation and our place in it. Those that have traveled to far lands, never known before, and to Jerusalem, have brought back new knowledge and new ideas; much more is known."

"In the time of our Holy Father Pius the Second," he continued, "it was thought that a boiling sea destroyed any ship that ventured past Cape Nun. Now, ships go all the way around Cape Good Hope and come into the Arabian Sea. We have spices from India and no longer believe there are rivers of gold or dragons or sheep as big as oxen in Africa," he added chuckling.

Janine laughed at his description, then, asked perceptively, "What is it that troubles you?"

He sat down on the grass beside her and was silent a minute, "Our Holy Church has seen many changes since the death of our Lord. And our Lord was not the only one crucified; it is said that two thousand others who rebelled against the rule of the Romans saw the same fate."

"Have you heard of the *Zealots*? No? A Pharisee rabbi named Judas of Galilee began the group. A *Zealot* revolt against Rome was overthrown and it is said that twenty thousand Jews were massacred at Caesarea. Finally, there was a massive exodus of Jews and Christ believers in the year of our Lord 135. Then, Emperor Hadrian had all Jews expelled from Judaea, and Jerusalem became a Roman city.

Shortly after that, Irenaeus wrote the *Five Books Against Heresies* proclaiming there could be only one valid Church and outside of that Church there could be no salvation. Anyone outside of this church was to be destroyed. Personal experience and personal union with the divine were completely denied and banned. This personal relationship, of course, would undermine the authority of the priests. His canon is essentially the book we have today. There were many believers two hundred years after our Lord, but in the Roman Empire, the state religion was sun worship. The cult of *Sol Invictus*, the Invincible Sun, came from Syria. Christians had held the Sabbath, or seventh day, as holy; now, they were forced to change to the Sun Day, because Emperor Constantine had declared the venerable day of the Sun to be the day of rest."

Janine listened intently, scarcely noticing that the cow was tugging at the rope.

Father Paolo continued, "Christians had celebrated the birth of our Lord in the month of January; now they changed their celebration to coincide with the festival of *Natalis Invictus* which was around December 25th when the rebirth of the sun caused the days to begin to grow longer." He paused.

"The previous Emperor, Diocletian, had attempted to destroy all Christian writings. Many had to be rewritten from memories, so when Constantine was converted to our Lord and convened the Council of Nicaea, he commissioned new copies of the Holy Book and sanctioned the destruction of all writings that did not agree with this council's opinion. They declared Jesus was a God, not a prophet. The Emperor allotted an income to the Church and installed the Bishop at Rome in the Lateran Palace. He declared him to be the "Vicar of Christ" and declared that he could delegate his power and had the right to anoint and depose kings. All monarchs were considered subservient to the Holy Father after this," continued Father Paolo.

"This Council condemned the teachings of Arius of Alexandria because he was proclaiming that Jesus was not divine, but a wholly mortal inspired teacher. Though it was condemned, King Constantine was somewhat sympathetic to this philosophy and after his son became king, Arianism all but displaced Christianity for quite awhile. In the four hundredth year after our Lord, almost every bishopric was Arian. When the Jews had been expelled from Jerusalem in the first century, many had settled in the south of the land of the Franks, this area, as we know it today. Many of the laws of these Teutonic tribes were taken directly from Judaic law, we see now. So, this Arianism became the dominant form of Christianity in South Franks and in the Pyrenees area of Catalonia and Castile. The Merovingian blood line rose to power here only to be overcome by the Visigoths, who sacked Rome but spared the Christian churches."

"Seven hundred years after the birth of our Lord" he continued, looking out over the valley, "the Muslims overran Spain, then Septimania and as far north as Lyon in our own Frankish territory. Charles of Martell pushed the Muslims back to Narbonne, but that city remained in Muslim hands with Jewish help. Charles vented his anger by devastating the countryside. Finally, Pepin, Charles' son, made a pact with the Jews and they turned against the Moors and let him into the city. They recognized him as king and validated his claim as a Jewish descendent, 'seed of the house of David,'" Father Paolo continued.

"Was he really of Jewish origin?" Janine asked.

"Apparently, for when the tribe of Benjamin had gone into exile long before the birth of Christ, many went to Arcadia and the city of Troy. From there, they migrated up the Danube River to the Teutonic tribes and intermarried. So, the lineage of Dagobert and Sigisbert were partially Israelite in origin. The men wore their hair long in acceptance of ancient traditions."

"Aside from all these wars, those faithful to the scripture as given by the Nicene Council continued to teach. As you know, St. Benedict gave us his Rule in 540 and in 597 St. Columbanus took a band of Irish monks into Brittany and Gaul. These black monks, as they were called then, were known for their obedience to their abbot and for their humility. As we know, this did not always remain the case as these monasteries became richer and more powerful. But, these monasteries did become centers of learning as well as religion and towns grew up around or near them."

Paolo paused to reflect. "In these times the barons were all-powerful over their areas. West Franks was made up of many of these small principalities and Roman rule was pushed out. These barons, who had many peasants on their lands, became the patrons and benefactors of the monasteries; and the concerns of the religious became their concerns. No one was concerned with the peasants; they couldn't even leave the manor without permission, so, many became outlaws, hiding in the forests." He paused and listened.

"Ah, Mother Marguerite is ringing the vespers bell; I have discoursed too long," Father Paolo ended abruptly. He took her hand and helped her to stand and took the rope of the cow, standing patiently nearby.

"You never said what was troubling you, Father," Janine reminded.

"I am trying to understand the actions that have been taken by our Church and its leaders, and bring this to accord with the words of Jesus," he replied.

"Yes, there have been times when I could not find peace or understand and was disturbed by the things I heard, but I just continued to love God and his creation and fulfill the duties of my vows. The other things became unimportant. But, of course, I have not read as widely as you nor have I seen as much in my limited travel," Janine said as they walked toward the stables.

"The passing ideas and postulates," Janine continued, "are like steps, one building upon another. But we continue to search for that purest truth."

He stopped abruptly and stared at her. She halted and looked into his eyes questioningly. "No?" she asked.

"Yes, yes, of course. That is a very wise observation. I have never known a woman of your age with such clarity of vision." he paused. "Yes, we keep searching." They walked on in silence.

Janine was somewhat uncomfortable knowing the looks that would come from Sister Jacqueline as they approached the *dormitorie* together, even though she knew their time had been quite innocent. Innocent, yes, but right now she wanted so badly to take his hand as they walked that she had to silently chide herself.

Chapter 8

Late Summer

Janine had become accustomed now to the routine of their convent and Father Paolo's schedule of late *vespers* and *compline* during the summer months. Evening prayers were after setting sun. Father Paolo was frequently helping someone in the village through the midday and at times going back to work after vespers until there was no light. Recently he had been helping Arnaud and Phillipe, the Benet brothers, in clearing a plot for farming. Janine had seen this done when she was a child and knew the hard chopping, digging and carrying involved. When Father Paolo was absent at their evening meal, Sister Jacqueline would keep his plate by the fireplace and carry it up to his cell as soon as she heard his door. Many times, she knew, he did not answer her knock.

Janine was busy in the garden and helping take care of *Madame* and the chickens at every spare minute between the offices, prayers and regular chores. She was happy from prayers at dawn till prayers beside her cot at bedtime. She hummed as she worked the soil around the cabbages, turnips, cress, radishes and carrots. She was especially watchful of the herb garden with parsley, thyme, sage and garlic. She had grown the beans and corn at St. Leonard but they had not grown well here this summer. During her work, she had given much thought to Father Paolo's discourse on history the day they sat under the tree. She wanted to learn more and she wanted to hear his opinions of the events.

She was beginning to realize that his education was more extensive than any person she had known, including her teachers at the convent. She read the scriptures, but many were not clear to her, even within Christ's teachings. When she finished her weeding, she walked through the meadow to the creek where *Madame's* bell was jingling occasionally. *Madame* was accustomed to her area now and never strayed very far, always returning when the vespers bell rang. But, Janine decided to bring her up after she had picked a large bouquet of wildflowers, which, of course, *Madame* wanted to eat. Janine laughed, "No, *Madame*, you have eaten flowers all day," and led her toward the stables.

She placed all the flowers but two in the chapel and was just going up the stairs when Mother Marguerite said, "Sister Janine, we do not adorn our cells; we offer all to God and keep our lives simple."

Janine bowed her head, went back and placed the flowers with the others in the vase. She then went to her place in the chapel and knelt. Her eyes were closed, but after a few moments, she sensed that someone had knelt beside her. As she peeked sideways, she met the crystal blue eyes of Father Paolo. He smiled gently then continued his prayers. She noticed that he was still in the habit that he wore for heavy work and was dusty and sweat-streaked. She felt a wonderful sense of calmness flow over her as she went back to her own prayers.

The vespers bell was ringing when she opened her eyes. When had he gone? In a few minutes, he appeared in fresh habit in his usual place and began the intonation.

At evening meal Father Paolo said, "Sisters, I have wonderful news! As you know, I have been trying for some time to get a grinding wheel for our little village. I have written many letters and have talked with all the villagers and now it is almost arranged. Pons and Jacotte and her ailing mother, Gaillarde, have not been able to provide well for themselves as bakers. Our village is too small and too poor. So, Pons has agreed to run the gristmill for a small fee from each family using the wheel. I have arranged with the Bishop for aid in buying an old wheel in *Clermont-Ferrand* and several of the villagers will help me to bring it down from the *massif.*"

"It is wonderful to see the villagers working together on a common goal. Now, we will not have to carry our grains to *Auben* for grinding. The Benet brothers also believe that rye and oats, and possibly, barley can be grown here. More clearing must be done on some of the land near the river that has not been farmed since the baroness died without heir and left these hectares to our holy Church. The bishop has agreed to a very small fee since much clearing and possibly dike building must be done. Several of the craftsmen have offered their help just to be involved along with the others. Of course, they want to see our village more prosperous for their own trades. There has even been some discussion of making a canal to bring water from the river to some of the farm plots. I see much more hopefulness here than when I first came to this village."

"That hopefulness is partly a result of the help you've given," said Mother Marguerite.

"Perhaps... I love these people, as do each of you," Father Paolo said, looking at each sister in turn. When his eyes met Janine's, they lingered; then he continued, "There is also sad news from the *massif* to the north of us. One of the barons was in bitter conflict with some neighbors on adjoining lands who were sympathetic to the Calvinists. It was said they were even holding services, which, of course, were banned by our King Henry and named a heresy by our Holy Father. Well, at any rate, the baron and his men set fire to the forests all around the lands of the Huguenot believers. The entire forest, which had been replanted years ago by the brothers of the Cistercian monastery, was burned. It is so sad when differing beliefs turn neighbors against each other. It's as though the Cathar heresy were happening again, but on a much wider scale. That, of course, was mostly in the Languedoc to the south of us. *Albi*, which is a day's ride by horse, was at the center of those ideas, and also the center of the Inquisition to stop them.

"What did the Cathari believe, Father?" asked Sister Janine.

"They believed God had created only the world of the spirit, the unseen, and that Satan created the material world. They felt that they must reject all possessions and live extremely simple lives, denying their own bodies even. They rejected the sacrament and the liturgy."

"Did not St. Francis also deny material possession and cling to the simple life, owning only his robe, underpants and cord?" asked Sister Jacqueline.

"Yes, his life was very ascetic; but he believed, as our Scripture says, that God created everything. The Cathar belief had come down through many centuries from the teachings of Mani, a royal Persian born near Baghdad about 200 years after the birth of our Lord. His followers even credited him with a virgin birth and called him Savior. He declared that he had received the same enlightenment as Jesus and it was said he could heal like Jesus. He wrote many books and believed that one is born and dies and is born and dies many times, over and over." He noted the looks of surprise and questioning around the table, but he went on, "Mani was imprisoned, flayed to death, skinned and decapitated."

"Oh!" He paused, frowning, noticing one nun sat with her hand over her mouth. "So sorry, Sister Jacqueline, I forget your delicate constitution." Jacqueline excused herself and went up the stairs to her cell.

He continued unperturbed, "This school of thought persisted in the Kingdom of Castile and spread out into Provence and Gaul. The excesses and, in some cases, immorality of our own clergy caused these ideas to gain popularity with the people in the twelfth century. Our Holy Father Innocent sent friars to preach, but they were not very successful. The Cathari believed that since the body was of Satan, that Christ did not come in the flesh and, therefore, was not killed and was, of course, not resurrected. . ." He paused, reflecting.

"So, the barons of Gaul in Auvergne organized a Crusade; and everyone who joined them was assured by holy offices of a place in heaven, remission of all sins and a canceling of penances. They had only to fight forty days and could also take all the goods they could plunder. Is my talk disturbing you, Mother Marguerite?" he asked as he noticed her silently crossing herself.

"No, Father," she replied, "I have at my age heard of many terrible things, but they still sadden me. If you will excuse me, I will help Sister Clare to her cot. I am very happy for the news about the gristmill. I will see you at *compline* prayers."

Father Paolo looked around with a smile, "I seem to have discoursed too lengthily again."

"No, Father Paolo, I would like to learn more about the history of our Church," Janine replied.

"Well, to finish my story, the culture of Provence was destroyed; the knights massacred many people, burned many towns and took over the lands. Much of the literature of this area was in the form of songs and fables kept alive by troubadours and traveling lyric poets. Our Church condemned those stories of chivalry and gallantry, as being immoral and decadent and most slowly vanished. There was much burning of books then, especially those that did not concur with the ideas of the reigning Pope.

"Was that not a good thing?" Janine asked as she began clearing the table.

"Since only you and I are here, I will say 'no, it was not good.' For much painstaking thought had been given to some of the postulates and might have helped others. But it was destroyed and lost and the next generation had not that step to build upon. As you said, 'One idea builds upon another.' When the snow comes, I will have more time for instruction and will talk with you more about some of those books."

"Sister Janine, the flowers in the chapel are very beautiful," he said and their eyes met again. Somehow, she knew from his look that he had overheard Mother Marguerite's rebuke.

"Consider the lilies of the field, they toil not, neither do they spin," Paolo quoted softly. "It is a gift to love and appreciate God's creation and want to share it," he said smiling.

Chapter 9

Early Fall

"Sisters! Father Paolo! Come quickly!" Janine shouted as she ran toward the refectory. Everyone was just gathering for the break fast. All but Sister Clare rushed outside.

"Our garden! It's been ravaged!" Janine mourned.

"The stupid cow probably got into it," said Sister Jacqueline wryly.

"No, someone has taken more than half of the cabbages and carrots and has trampled on many of the herbs," Janine observed. "*Madame* is in her stable."

Father Paolo walked around carefully inspecting the grounds. "There were several people here, at least three; one had bare feet. Sister Janine, it was probably a small band of homeless just passing through the area. As our Lord said, 'him that takes your cloak, forbid him not to take your coat also. Behold the fowls of the air, for they sow not, neither do they reap, nor gather into barns, yet your heavenly Father feeds them.' We shall have plenty. Come, now, let us express thankfulness at our table for that which we do have this day."

Janine lingered a few moments, straightening a plant here and there, then followed the others inside, looking a little sad. Today, she decided, would be a good time to begin storing the vegetables in the grotto under the bell tower.

Clouds were darkening the sky as Janine carried the beautiful cabbages to the underground cave. She had worked through her usual chores as quickly as she could, rearranged the shelves in the cellar and swept off the steps. The cellar needed to be aired, but the clouds were threatening rain. Janine took her candle to the back of the cave to stack more shelves on the square rocks. As she set down the candle, her foot struck something and she bent to examine it. It was a large pouch full of gold coins. This seemed very unusual - not the customary tidy style of Father Paolo. He was very businesslike in his accounting of the pittance given to the Church by the parishioners. Well, it was none of her concern or interest, she decided. Her concern today was storing the carrots and turnips. As she went up the steps, she noticed a fine mist had begun to fall. Working furiously, she managed to get all the vegetables cleaned and stored before the vespers bell rang. She was soaked to the skin; her habit felt as if it weighed ten times what it should. She sneezed as she put the large water kettle on the hook and began building up the fire.

"Sister Janine, look at you! Where have you been?" asked Jacqueline.

"I've put the vegetables in the cellar, Sister," Janine replied, sneezing again.

"Well, I had no idea. I was in my room," said Jacqueline.

Janine looked at her incredulously, but said nothing, just shook her head.

"So . . . you were in the grotto?" asked Jacqueline. "What is it like? I've never been there; I'm not very fond of caves."

"It is just a cellar," said Janine unenthusiastically.

The next day as Janine scrubbed the floors of the nave, she heard footsteps behind her.

"Sister Janine, come with me," said Father Paolo. "Sister Jacqueline will finish here. Mother Marguerite said we must further your teachings if we are to have a school here soon, and I believe I am qualified. The rain continues so I am unable to help in the village with the new grinding wheel."

Janine rose slowly, dried her hands and brushed off her habit. She followed the priest through the refectory to the back stairway. Sister Jacqueline sent a look of pure contempt at her as they passed. Janine just shook her head and tried to dismiss it from her mind as she climbed the stairs. Father Paolo's room was large with windows on the north and west overlooking part of the valley. One was shuttered against the cold rain falling steadily. Books were stacked on one side of the large table.

He drew up a comfortable chair for her and sat down in what appeared to be his usual place at the table. A crackling noise drew her attention to a small fire burning in the fireplace. He sat for a moment looking at her. She raised her eyes to his and smiled, then dabbed at her nose with her handkerchief.

"Your sneezes are worse today," Paolo observed.

"Yes, Father, but they will be gone soon. I am drinking a tea of herbs," she replied.

"Well, where shall we begin?" he asked. "History of our holy Church, theology or the teachings of our Lord Jesus?"

"I have much to learn, Father. May I speak of one thing first though?" asked Janine. "Sister Clare grows worse, especially with this rain. If she could be taken to the hot springs that flow in the area of the mountains near Clermont-Ferrand, her pain might be eased."

"Do you think she could undertake that kind of journey?" he asked.

"I don't know; maybe, if the weather were warmer," she replied.

"Perhaps in a covered coach," Father Paolo said slowly, thinking. "I will see if something can be arranged. In that same area, you may have heard, the Chapel of *Saint-Michel d' Arguilhe* in *Le Puy* was built right on the ruins of a Roman temple dedicated to Mercury."

"No," she replied, "I wasn't aware of that, but the town of Limoges also had its beginnings in the Roman times. It was known then as *Augustorium* and a great amphitheatre was built there."

"Yes, I have heard of it, and I have seen the sacrificial alter that the Romans built in the square at Taine, used to worship the pagan gods. Only seventy years before the birth of our Lord, His country fell to the Roman army under Pompey. The kings that they placed there to rule were from Arabia and a heavy taxation was placed on the people. The torture used in their courts and trials led many to take their own lives. Though our own scriptures do not mention it, other writings reveal that Pontius Pilot was very corrupt and very cruel. The writings that were authorized by our Council later, could not say this, for they were still under the rule of Roman Emperor Constantine. The Jews had hoped that Jesus would lead them in being liberated from Rome. That is why they called Him - Messiah - anointed king. But His mission, of course, was one of spirit."

"It has been said that He was a student in one of the Essene communities. The Essenes believed that one experienced pure knowing through a mystical relationship with God and this experience gave them freedom. They taught that one must look for the 'light' within - the revelation, the knowing, and not look to others to lead them to God. There are writings by one known as Valentinus, who lived about a hundred years after the death of our Lord, that allege that Jesus taught certain secrets and mysteries of this sort to his closest disciples. Most of what we know about Valentinus comes from the writings of Bishop Irenaeus of Lyon in the Rhone Valley, around the year 180. The books Valentinus wrote were denounced as heretical during the reign of Constantine, who was, as you probably know, the first Roman Emperor to be converted to Christ. Most of these books were burned though some may remain hidden. It is rumored that the monastery of *St. Pachomius* in the upper part of Egypt had copies of many of the works of heresy but they were never found."

"When the apostles were yet alive, all believers shared the same teachings, shared their money and property and all worshiped together. As the believers scattered to all parts of the world due to the Roman persecution, the teaching became more and more diverse as it encountered many different cultures and was adapted. Within a hundred years, many slightly different doctrines were being taught. At that time, there were numerous gospels, writings and secret teachings circulating, perhaps over a hundred. And hundreds of teachers claimed to teach the true doctrine. Valentinus was a poet and claimed to have learned St. Paul's secret teachings from Theudas, one of the saint's own disciples. From our own Scriptures we know that St. Paul was caught up in an ecstatic trance and that he was told things that cannot be told - hidden mysteries and secret wisdom. The followers of Valentinus claimed to have these secret teachings. These followers, called Gnostics because they claimed to possess this secret knowledge, were accused of fraud and heresy by Bishop Irenaeus, who said 'they even admit nothing supports their claim but intuition. They say that 'whoever has not known himself, has known nothing, but whoever has known himself has simultaneously achieved knowledge about the depth of all things.' The Bishop complained that among these Gnostics, one was not considered mature or initiated unless he shared some new insight or 'enormous fiction' as the Bishop called them."

"Heracleon who was a student of Valentinus said, 'at first, people believe because of the testimony of others, but then they come to believe from the Truth itself.' Bishop Irenaeus, of course, disagreed with this vehemently, saying that the apostles 'placed in the Church everything that belongs to truth so that everyone can draw from her the water of life.'"

"But the heretics felt the Church had gone far beyond the original teachings of the apostles. Having received the secret knowledge themselves, they felt they were wiser than the apostles and, of course, wiser than the priests."

Janine looked at Father Paolo with a slight expression of shock. He just laughed and said, "I am not telling you this to confuse you. But I see that you are wiser and more directly in tune with the mystical nature of life and I want you to know that many others have had these mystical experiences and just because they were named heretics by a council does not necessarily mean that they were wrong. There are many who God shines His light on that have never heard of our Holy Church."

A movement near the partially opened door caught Janine's attention and she turned to look at the doorway. The priest's eyes followed hers. She looked back at him questioningly. He silently stepped to the door, looked around, and then closed the door softly.

"Just Sister Jacqueline, snooping again. She probably wanted to see if I was experiencing 'carnal knowledge' with you as she has hinted that she wants with me."

Janine looked at him, her eyes wide with shock. She couldn't seem to speak.

"I'm sorry, it was wrong of me to disclose that," he said apologetically, "but I felt you might understand the difficulty it puts upon me."

"Of course . . . I . . . ah . . . do," she stammered, then went on slowly. "The allegiance to vows is something I also have had much thought about recently. We are taught chastity, obedience and poverty, but Our Lord taught that the greatest service and greatest virtue is love. Love is always acceptable to God. My vow was that my body would be given wholly in God's service. St. Francis felt that the body was to be denied, kept under strict control, disciplined and castigated. To you only I will say, that I differ some in my feeling about our bodies. There is a reason for our bodies; the Scriptures say it is the temple of God. We are more than just spirit and to deny the body and try to live only in the contemplative spirit life is to deny the existence God has placed us in. Living fully, enjoying the warmth of 'Brother Sun' and the beauty of 'Sister Moon', the flowers, the voices in hymns, the food God gives us, all prepares us to then live fully in the spirit when that time comes to us."

Her eyes met his for a long time and they both smiled. "I feel the same," he said softly, "but I have never heard it put more beautifully."

"Well now," he continued, "back to early heresies and the early Church." He paused, thinking. "Those who disagreed with Bishop Irenaeus claimed that St. Peter had written that the risen Christ had revealed to him that those who call themselves bishops and deacons are waterless canals. The followers of Valentinus were opposed to an institutional framework and believed that those who had received gnosis, or secret knowledge, had transcended the authority of a hierarchy. Direct personal contact with the living Christ took precedence over any tradition for them. They claimed to offer every initiate direct access to God. Valentinus spoke of God as 'the Root of All, the Ineffable One who dwells alone in silence, the Ultimate Source of All Being, the Depth.' Our Bishops referred to God as the Judge, a King, or as a Master or Father. The Gnostics spoke of God as He who is pre-existent, the divine Father-Mother. As Valentinus said, 'God is indescribable but can be imagined as the great male/female power, Primal Father and Grace, Silence, the Womb and Mother of all. He claimed that Jesus spoke of 'my Mother, the Spirit' and his divine Father, the Father of Truth.'"

"Every one of the texts that referred to God as sexless or both sexes were branded heretical and by the time the process of sorting all the writings was completed nearly two hundred years after our Lord's death, this feminine side of God had disappeared. Bishop Irenaeus expressed dismay that many women, even in the Rhone district, were attracted to these Gnostic teachings. He said that Marcus, another student of Valentinus, addressed his prayers to Grace, She who is before all things, and to Wisdom and Silence, the feminine element of the divine being. Marcus encouraged women to prophesy, which, of course, was strictly forbidden in the early Church. In the Gnostic meetings, there was no distinction or rank between men and women. All present, including the women, drew lots and whoever received a certain lot was designated as the priest on that day; another was to read the Scripture and others would address the group as prophets. This drawing would occur at each meeting so that roles continually changed. They followed the principle of strict equality, believing that since God directs everything, the way the lots fell expressed His choices. Irenaeus ended his treatise by saying, 'Let those who blaspheme the Creator, as the Valentinians and all the falsely so-called Gnostics, be recognized as agents of Satan.' Actually, many whom he censured for supporting Gnostic teachings were prominent members of the Church. One revered father of the Church, Clement of Alexandria, writing in Egypt, wrote that 'men and women are to receive the same instruction, for in Christ, there is neither male nor female.'"

"However, his views were not widely accepted; the majority went with Tertullian who reiterated that it is not permitted for a woman to teach, or baptize, nor share in the priestly office. So, you can see that there was much dissension among those who professed to follow the teachings of Christ. But their common danger was from their Roman rulers who demanded that they renounce Christ entirely and swear by the genius of the Emperor and offer sacrifices to their pagan gods. If Christians were arrested and refused to do this, they were tortured and killed."

"From the time of Emperor Nero, 20 years after the death of our Lord until the reign of Constantine, three hundred years later, the persecution was savage. Tacitus, who was a Roman historian, and Josephus, a Jewish historian, both wrote about those early conflicts. In the second century, Justin, a Christian philosopher, spoke out against these persecutions to Emperor Antonius and the Emperor's son, Marcus Arelius, but he met with the same fate as Ptolemy and all of their students. Even the Bishop Polycarp of Smyrna, who was the teacher of Bishop Irenaeus, was not spared. Many who professed Christ were tortured to death in the public arena, beheaded, or burned alive. Wild beasts were turned on some tied to posts in the arena. This was after they had been whipped and forced to sit on an iron seat over a fire, to try to make them swear by pagan idols."

"Why was there so much cruelty and violence?" Janine asked.

"I cannot guess why some act the way they do. Our beloved St. Francis never upheld this kind of behavior. Even in Lyon, our own nearby city, during the time of Irenaeus, Christians were prohibited from entering the markets or the baths. Around Vienne, mobs attacked the Christians, some were beaten or stoned, and many were dragged into the Forum, accused and thrown into prison. At the Roman holiday of summer, the Governor offered the torture and execution of Christians in the arena as entertainment. Nearly fifty had died in a two-month period one summer, among them the ninety year old Bishop Pothinus who died of torture and exposure in prison."

"It was at that time that Irenaeus was persuaded to take over the position of Bishop. He seemed more opposed to the Gnostics than the pagans though. The Gnostics believed that only the human element suffered, that the divine spirit transcended the suffering. So, to suffer as a martyr did not necessarily mean that the spirit had undergone any enlightenment. But, of course, we know that many more people have felt closer to that human Jesus because He did suffer what they suffer in the body. So, the Gnostics felt that one must 'end the sleep,' come out of the darkness," Father Paolo said quoting, "'bring forth what is in you for what you bring forth will save you, what you do not bring forth will destroy you.' They spoke of finding one's true identity and that the Kingdom of God is inside of you: a state of self-discovery, a time when opposites become the same thing. Our Gospel of Luke proclaims, 'The Kingdom of God is within you.' The Gnostics said, 'Every one of you who has known himself has seen the pure light.' And 'the one who seeks the truth is also the one who reveals it.' They suggested that one learns what he needs to know by himself in meditative silence. Our own St. Francis spoke of the active - contemplative life. He encouraged his followers to find solitude, reaching a state of absolute inner silence, to quiet all thoughts, dispel all ideas, and give themselves up to meditation. The Gnostics said, 'Entrust yourself to God alone as father and friend' and also, 'you saw the spirit, you became the spirit, you saw the Christ, you became the Christ.' Of course, anyone with this perspective would not recognize the structure of the Holy Church and its bishops, priests and rituals as being necessary."

"When I hear of the Huguenots and the followers of Calvin, I am reminded of these Gnostics. Though not fully the same, this new teaching encourages each person to be his own priest and go to God directly. They substitute the inner authority of conscience for the external authority of the Church. I have heard there is a group of these believers in *Montauban* and another even nearer in *Sauveterre*. King Henry's edict of *Chateaubriant* prohibited their meetings, but their numbers continue to grow. One of these, whose name is *Condé*, is demanding liberty of conscience."

"With the death of King Henry at the tournament two summers ago, there has been an attempt to make peace with these Calvinists but the Bishops, exercising their right to try the heretics by Inquisition methods, have kept the passions flaring. The death of young King Francis last winter has put the authority with his son and the queen-mother, Catherine dé Medici and she has tried to pacify each side and keep the peace. It is said that a charter of enfranchisement may be given. But, I fear the Duke of Guise will not abide by this, and there will be more blood shed in the name of our Lord," he sighed.

There was a knock at the door. "Come in Mother Marguerite. Yes, I have been talking and not noticed that it is time for the *nones* bell," he said, without her even speaking. "Please see that Sister Janine drinks the tea of the bayberry bark and coltsfoot; her cough seems worse. Oh yes, Sister Janine, here is a book about Irenaeus to study," he said, handing her a large volume. "I will be away for three days but we will continue instruction when I return."

Early Fall

There had been very little conversation during the evening meal, except for Father Paolo's sharing that the Abbot sent his blessings to all. "Where is Sister Janine?" he asked.

"She has been in her cell for two days, her cough is much worse," replied Mother Marguerite.

"I have lit a candle for her," said Sister Clare.

He looked up quickly with a questioning glance at Sister Clare. Clare nodded her head.

"Come with me, Mother Marguerite!" he demanded and bounded up the stairs.

"This is most unusual," Marguerite said softly, fluttering along behind him.

He pushed open the door of Janine's cell. "When did you last check on her?"

"She seemed to be sleeping when I peeked in at *nones* bell," replied Marguerite.

"Dear Lord, she is scarcely breathing," he said bending over the inert body. "Why is it so cold in here? Must these doors always be closed?" he demanded.

"Well, you know our custom," she answered weakly.

"Sister Janine, can you hear me?" he called out. Her eyes rolled weakly and closed again.

"Bring the blankets. I will take her downstairs!" he barked.

"This is most unusual," she began, but was cut short by a look from Father Paolo that clearly said, "no more."

As he gently picked up Janine, the blankets fell off. She laid her head against his shoulder. He could not help but notice the perfection of her body through the plain white gown and the shining long brown hair that fell across her face and his arm. He would have been stirred almost beyond control had he not been so afraid for her life. He had seen these cases at the *hôpital* in Paris when the breathing was stopped by so much congestion in the chest.

He carried her down the narrow stairs and laid her on Sister Clare's cot. Sister Jacqueline's only help was an exclamation of shock as he carried Janine through the refectory where she was still seated. He dashed back up the stairs and brought down Janine's wooden cot and *materas*. He placed them near the fireplace. Sister Clare hobbled over and placed a soft blanket on the bed while Father Paolo quickly went to Clare's cell and lifted Janine again. She was so weak her head fell back and he was almost overcome with a desire to touch her lips with his. He placed her gently on the cot and Mother Marguerite placed the blankets around her.

"Sister Jacqueline, go to my room and bring the little box on the table marked 'black willow,'" he ordered. "Sister Clare, do you have some soft cloths for poultice?"

"Yes, of course, Father," replied Sister Clare, shuffling off quicker than he had seen her move lately.

"Mother Marguerite, please place the kettle and the teapot over the fire," he requested as he darted into the kitchen and began searching through the cans of herbs.

"Have we any wild cherry bark?" he shouted.

Sister Clare replied, "I believe Sister Janine was still curing it in her cell."

He dashed up the stairs again and back down again with a handful of the bark. "Sister Jacqueline, please bring the grinding bowl and pestle, oh, and a large bowl also," he requested, noting her raised eyebrows and scowl.

He placed a handful of the mustard seeds in the bowl she brought and began grinding vigorously, mixing in the bits of bark and leaves of comfrey. He added the boiling water and made a thick paste. "Sister Clare, please fold the cloths and then pour boiling water over them in the large bowl."

Going to the cot near the fireplace, he said, "Now, Mother Marguerite, please untie her gown and fold it back," he said. He took a handful of the mush and placed it on her chest, smoothing it from her throat to the top of her round breasts. "Now, the bowl, please, Sister Clare," he requested. Mother Marguerite flinched as she watched him take the cloths from the scalding water. He wrung them gently, held them till he was satisfied the temperature was just right, and then placed them over the poultice. He replaced her gown and blankets. Her eyes fluttered, but she did not move.

"Now, all of you, off to prayers. Thank you for your help. I will stay," Father Paolo said. He caught Jacqueline's look of scorn as she turned away.

He went to the kitchen, found the leftover broth and set it by the fireplace, carried in more wood then gently checked the warmth of the poultice. He placed his arm under Janine's neck and said softly, "Janine, can you sip a little of this borage tea?" Her eyes fluttered, but could not seem to open. He held the cup to her lips and smiled as she took a little. Then she began coughing. "Good, good," he said, "that must all be coughed out." He laid her back gently.

As each cloth cooled, he put on a fresh warm one. Once he was able to get her to sip a little broth. He sat on the bench by the fireplace and scarcely noticed when the nuns went to their rooms.

As the night wore on, with Janine not responding, he knelt beside her cot and prayers tumbled out of his heart from a depth he had never felt before. He did not know how long he had been kneeling when he was aware of a movement. Janine weakly raised herself on one elbow and looked at him, questioningly, uncomprehendingly at first. She struggled to sit up, and then, gracefully slid to her knees on the floor beside him. He watched with astonishment, thinking he was dreaming. He pulled the blanket around her white shoulders and silently went back to prayers with her beside him. The rain had finally ceased and the moonlight fell across the floor touching their feet.

Chapter 10

Early Winter

"Through this holy anointing and His most tender mercy, may the Lord forgive you whatever sins you have committed by the sins of sight, hearing, smell, taste and speech, touch and steps. Amen," intoned Father Paolo, touching with the holy oil the eyes, ears, nose, mouth, fingertips and toes of the dying one.

Gaillarde's daughter, Jacotte, wept silently by the bed. He handed the anointing oil to Mother Marguerite who had risen from her knees.

Taking the holy wafer and placing it in the mouth of the dying woman, he said, "Receive sister Gaillarde, the viaticum of the Body of Our Lord Jesus Christ. May He guard thee from the malignant foe and lead thee to eternal life." He had not imagined that so many of the friends and relatives could fit into a small house such as this one of Pons and Jacotte. His thoughts were of these many good people as he finished the ceremony of extreme unction. What were their hopes, fears, questions? He knew many of their confessed sins. Were their concerns the same as his? He gently took the hand of each person before he left the house.

"And they cast out many devils, and anointed with oil many that were sick and healed them, Saint Mark," quoted Father Paolo as he and Marguerite walked toward the church. "Where is the healing, Mother Marguerite?" he asked.

"That is God's part," she replied. "And we have seen healing," she said, looking at him with shining eyes.

"Yes, we still give thanks for Sister Janine's recovery," he agreed. "But what are we doing here, Mother?" he asked.

"You are asking very difficult questions today, Father," she said smiling. "We are here because God wants us to be here and also because we chose this path."

"But, are we doing any good? Are we helping others to find God? Are we really fulfilling God's will?" he asked.

"Father Paolo, you do not know the despair and wretchedness that were in this village before you came. I speak in confidence. The one who was before you lowered the morals and the spirits of all the people more than I've seen anywhere in all my service. There are two young women I know of who still have not been able to free themselves from the passions he taught. They yet sell their bodies freely. But the help and guidance you have given in one year have pulled this village back out of the mire and set it before God. I know not one person who has taken after this new heresy."

"Thank you for your comfort, Mother Marguerite," he replied.

"We all have our days of unrest, Father. Those are days for longer prayers," she responded.

"Is Sister Janine well enough for more instruction?" he asked. He noticed her long pause before she answered.

"Yes, she is well enough in body, but there has been some change in her. She is even quieter than before and spends even more time in prayer. I feel she is having a time of unrest also. Please keep in mind this fragileness of spirit and her burdens, whatever they may be, at this time."

"Yes, I will, and thank you again, Mother, for sharing your insights with me," he said as they entered the chapel.

Janine was kneeling in her usual place. The soft glow of the sanctuary candles fell across her face and the priest could not help but gaze at her, after Mother Marguerite had closed her eyes in prayer. His thoughts went back to the family in grief. When

Gaillarde died, he knew the family would keep a few locks of her hair and trimmings of the fingernails and toenails to 'preserve the *domus*.' The old superstitions of sustaining the good fortune of the household were still strong. How did these ideas get started? The joyous celebration of the birth of the Lord would be soon. Was this great celebration that much different from these local superstitions or the celebration of the Sun in Roman days when the common people believed that their celebration caused the sun to stop getting weaker and begin being with them longer each day? The Jews had yet other kinds of offerings to God. The Muslims believed that they must pray toward Mecca five times a day. Mohammed had written of only one God and had spoken of Jesus as a prophet many times in his writings. He claimed to have had direct revelation from God in the many visions he had while in a cave. Father Paolo realized his thoughts were not on his prayers and began again.

"This is delicious. What was that you sprinkled in the tea?" Janine asked.

"It is the ground bark from a tree that grows in the countries far to the east and the ground seed from another plant, also from the land of mysteries," replied Father Paolo.

"It is wonderful with the honey. Are these like the precious sweet spices that are spoken of in the scriptures that Mary Magdalene brought to the tomb of the Savior on the day after the Sabbath?" Janine asked.

"It could be. It is not known," he replied. "King Solomon also spoke of spices and spiced wine. Spices, almond paste, figs and dates were brought first to our country by the crusaders returning from the country of our Lord's birth. The Arabian merchants have traded with the East for many hundred years."

He sat down at the table across from her and sipped at the tea, apparently lost in thought. "Where shall we begin?" he pondered out loud. "We talked about the persecution of the land of Israel. The temple in Jerusalem was plundered by the Roman legions under Emperor Titus. The Romans had come even into Gaul here, established towns, and had built many stone bridges, some that we still use. Gaul was fully under Roman rule fifty years before the birth of Christ. . . ." He paused in thought. "And we spoke of Ptolemy who lived in Egypt a hundred years after the birth of our Lord and wrote *Geographia* and about music and astronomy. You know about astronomy?" he asked.

Janine nodded her head affirmatively so he went on. "And we spoke at length about Irenaeus who wrote the *Five Books Against Heresies* declaring there could be no salvation outside the Church. He was especially wrathful of the Valentinian Gnostics who believed salvation was attained in personal experience and personal union with the divine. Epiphanius of Salamis also wrote a treatise on heresies about two hundred years later, specifically about Arius, who, he said, was a Libyan and schooled in Antioch by Lucian. Since Arius taught that Jesus the Son was a created being, not God, he and his followers were excommunicated at the Council of Nicea under Roman king, Constantine. The council refuted the Arian claim by saying, 'the Son was of the same substance with the Father,' thus not created nor subordinate to Him. Arius was exiled in Illyria but in the year 330 he was recalled and was to be received by the King in Constantinople. However, he was taken by a sudden illness and died within hours."

"During this time there were hermit groups of Christians called *lavras* who lived in a communal manner. They were usually self-supporting by means of farming or crafts and divided their days between prayer, work and meditative reading. In our area, these groups were very disliked by the landowners and even the bishops. One of the first of these groups was near Poitiers. This philosophy spread to England and Ireland and the Low Countries. It required great austerity, fasting and immersion in cold water to discipline the body. There was no leader or rule, just wandering teachers." Paolo paused. "This sounds like Saint Francis, doesn't it?" he said smiling. She smiled and nodded.

"The hermit groups were the beginning of our monasteries as we know them today. These were men of wisdom and perception. One was a Greek named Evagrius who lived in the last half of the fourth century. He said, 'The end of our profession is the kingdom of God, but our immediate aim is purity of heart. It is impossible for a man hindered by the fragile body to cleave always to God and be united with Him inseparably in contemplation, but it behooves us to know whither to direct our soul's intent.'" he quoted.

"That's very beautiful. I had never heard it. How do you remember it all?" Janine asked.

"I love the history of our Church and I studied many years. You are familiar with the Rule of Benedict of Nursia, which came a hundred years after Evagrius, yes? As an abbot, he made the rule for his monks and it was so excellent it eventually was used widely. There was, as you know, emphasis on charity and the harmony of a simple life. 'The care of the sick shall come above all else,' St. Benedict said, quoting Jesus. 'I was sick and you visited me; what you have done to one of these little ones you have done to me.' There was much chaos and turmoil at this time in almost every land. Kingdoms were changing rulers; great estates were being broken up, so the monastery, being self-sufficient, usually escaped peril when towns were destroyed in the wars. So they grew to include, as we know, the *hôpitals*, schools, courts, storehouses and libraries."

"But to get back to Rome," he continued. "The Council of Nicaea convened by King Constantine decided by vote that Jesus was a god, not a mortal prophet. The celebration of Pascaltide was established. Diocletian, the king before Constantine, had attempted to destroy all Christian writings, but of those saved, the Council decided which ones were to be accepted. Then a year later, Constantine sanctioned the destruction of those writings that the Council had not accepted or which challenged their beliefs. Then, he commissioned copies to be made of this accepted Scripture. And this is what we have yet today."

Father Paolo continued, "The Basilica at St. Peter's tomb was started during the reign of Constantine also. It was an enormous project because the tomb was on a hillside and much earth had to be moved from the high side to the low side to level the area. The wall on the south side was the height of six men when finished. Apparently, the Altar was placed in front of the shrine on holy days. The building was of brick and timber but many offerings of precious metalwork, jewels, sculptured marble and frescoes were brought to adorn it. It has been plundered again and again, first by Alaric the Goth, then Attila, king of the Huns, in the year of our Lord 452. Apparently, the tomb was spared by the Visigoths in 480, but not by the Saracens nearly 400 years later. Each time, the shrine was repaired by the devout. Pope Gregory instructed that the altar be placed on a platform so that with the lowering of the tomb, mass could be celebrated over the tomb."

"It was just about this same time that Mohammed was recording his 'Moments of Illumination' in short verses. His message was of One God who is infinite, imminent and 'closer to a man than the vein of his neck,' merciful and compassionate. I would agree with at least that part of his description of God, wouldn't you?"

"Yes, of course, but he also taught that our Lord was only a prophet," replied Janine.

"Well, at any rate, these verses are some of the earliest pieces of Arabic literature that we have. These Muslim believers conquered Spain and came into Septimania and it took Christians 700 years to retake some of these areas.

"But to get back to our area; the abbeys were growing and many had large tracts of land. There began to be a great interest in the literatures of the world. The bishops censored many books but allowed copying and illuminating of some of the texts, and many abbeys had large libraries.

Around this time a monk named Bede who lived in Yorkshire wrote about one of the abbots, 'He remained so humble and like the other brethren that he took pleasure in threshing and winnowing, milking the ewes and cows and employed himself in the bakehouse, the kitchen and the garden.' Bede said this abbot followed the advice of a wise man, who said, 'Be amongst them like one of them, gentle, affable and good to all.' Bede's life has been the greatest example to me other than our Lord and our St. Francis whom this quote might describe also."

"In the year 395 the Great Roman Empire was divided into the eastern empire ruled from Constantinople and the western part ruled from Rome. In less than a hundred years, the western empire collapsed. Various barbarian kingdoms took portions and trade declined drastically. Travel was very dangerous everywhere. The monasteries were about the only stable and peaceful safe places at that time.

Our area was called West Franks or Gaul and was ruled by powerful barons who made their own laws and were accountable to no one. But they were instrumental in establishing ports on the coasts and supporting the Church and its monasteries. As time went on, the Holy Roman Empire, not to be confused with the empire ruled from Rome in an earlier period, to the east grew larger and larger under Pippin and his son Charlemagne. This empire extended into the Low Countries to the Elbe River on the north and, at one time, as far south as Ebro in Castile across the Pyrenees. In the late 700s, Charlemagne, at the request of Pope Adrian, conquered the Lombard Kingdom north of Rome and the duchy of Bavaria. His greatest threat, though, was from the Saxons to the east, the Avars of Hungary, and the Slavs and Danes who attacked from leathern boats across the North Sea."

"In the year of our Lord 800, the Frankish army had restored Pope Leo III to Rome after a revolt the previous year. He had a silver *baldacchino* constructed and on Christmas Eve before the tomb of St. Peter, the Holy Father placed the imperial crown on Charlemagne's head. At the great assembly of *Aix la Chapelle* two years later Charlemagne demanded an oath of allegiance from all there to himself as Caesar."

"He was buried there twelve years later and no monarch following him could hold this vast empire together. His successors were weak; so, many parcels were seized by dukes and noblemen. The Vikings stepped up their attacks from the north. There was some decline of the monasteries around this time, but then in 910, the abbey at Cluny was built and the abbot subjected it to the Church of St. Peter in Rome. After that, each new abbey that was founded or accepted by it lost its independence and became obedient to the abbot at Cluny. These abbeys were not disturbed by any noble or lord. Cluny had over 300 monks. As time went on there was a lot of self-indulgence and splendor in some of these abbeys; more and more time was spent in offices and services until manual labor was almost non-existent. There was no time for it.

The hermit groups continued to exist however. The Cistercians was one group that dropped some of the elaborate ceremony and practiced pastoral farming with lay brothers. They, of course, were known as the 'white monks.' I'm sure you know much of this, but I am trying to bring it all into the whole of history at that time," Father Paolo said.

"Yes, Father, but I do appreciate the time you are taking to help me understand it," Janine replied.

"The Cistercian numbers grew as well as the black monks, but many abbots became vassals of the king. So, there was some dissension between the King and the Church. In 1092, King Phillip was excommunicated for a bigamous marriage, but, at length, he was absolved upon pretense of separation from one. It was around that time that many of our great cathedrals such as Notre Dame and Chartres were finished. Henry II, King of England owned more land by inheritance in Gaul than did our own king. In 1095, the Great Council met in Clermont and Pope Urban appealed to all to help liberate Jerusalem from the Muslims. When this crusade began, there was no discipline and few weapons. Some princes and noblemen joined but they were not well prepared either. Famine and sickness spread through the ranks and most of those left were killed in the siege of Jerusalem that lasted forty days. They broke through on the day of Passion after one monk had a vision and claimed to find the head of the spear that had pierced the Savior's side.

Muslim men, women and children were killed. Jews were burned in their synagogue and there was a lot of looting. After the victory, some of the Frankish dukes and lords were placed in power; and, after meeting with one of these nobles, The Count of Champagne went to Jerusalem and stayed for four years. Later, nine knights of his acquaintance or family joined him and were given a wing in the palace. The Count donated much of his lands to the Cistercians, whose spokesmen were St. Bernard and his uncle, *Andre de Montbard*. It is said that their horses were stabled in the Stables of Solomon under the Temple. This group came to be known as the Knights Templar. In 1128, the Church Council at Troyes recognized the order as a religious-military order and it expanded rapidly and amassed great wealth. In 1139, Pope Innocent II who was a protégé of St. Bernard declared the Templars would be independent and have no allegiance except to the Pope. They adopted the red cross *pattée* as their symbol. During this time, the Knights were engaged in the diplomacy between kings of the various realms and established much of the exchange of finances and banking between countries. They helped establish the Teutonic Order to defend the Holy Land but this order eventually settled in Prussia and overran that country with utmost savagery."

"Around the end of that century, the Muslims under Saladin took Jerusalem again but they granted the Christian survivors safe passage back to their countries. The great cross was taken down and dragged through the mire for two days. So, the Crusaders main goal of freeing the Christian shrines from the Muslims and restoring them as centers of pilgrimage had, in the end, failed.

"However, in 1192 there was a truce and unarmed pilgrims were allowed to visit the Holy Sepulchre. This was a very low time in the history of our Church - the bishops were being appointed by each country's leaders, most of the clergy was not celibate, the monasteries seemed only interested in accumulating wealth, and there was much criticism from the people on these last two issues. The Cathari heresy was spreading. Abbot Conrad of Mondsee was murdered by some nobles for trying to reclaim some possessions of his abbey."

"However, some good changes were happening. In the breaking up of some of the estates, many peasants were able to buy or gain their freedom and many towns were buying charters to self govern. The crusaders brought home new ideas as well as new products. Silk, velvet and brocade, mirrors and aromatic scents became more common, as did bathing. The crusaders, though mostly seeking wealth and power, had seen the educational centers of the Arabs, their use of opium and myrrh in surgery, and their making of paper from cotton.

"In 1204 the crusaders marched on Constantinople, vowing to bring those of the eastern split back into the Roman Church. They burned priceless paintings, manuscripts and treasures, but in the end, the Greeks would not yield to the Latin Church. These wars were the saddest kind, but there was a broadening of perception and knowledge and new fields of inquiry opened. Fairs and markets became regular places for exchange of goods between farmers and towns and other countries. And the great universities came into being to disperse this new knowledge."

"Of course, by this time the wind mills and water mills that were used in Syria sprang up all over our country and the neighboring provinces. Then appeared Francis of Assisi and Dominic the Spaniard, but that story will have to wait for another day," concluded Father Paolo. "From the smells floating up the stairway, I would guess that Mother Marguerite has made her wonderful bread and poached fish, such as our Lord gave to his audience of four thousand on the hill by the Sea of Galilee."

"Sister Janine, I have noticed you have been eating very little lately. Are you well? I would be sad if you became ill again," he asked.

"No, Father, I am just fine. I have had new thoughts to deal with since my sickness. I do not know if I can tell even you what I saw before you brought me down to the fireplace," Janine paused.

"Please, go on, you know that I've seen many things and always try to understand them," he entreated.

She raised her eyes to his, "Yes, you do. Well, as I remember, my breathing became most difficult; I was burning hot, then shaking cold. Then I felt I was drifting off to sleep and felt warm and comfortable. I seemed to be floating or flying like a butterfly; I felt so free. Then there was a soft radiant light all around and I floated further. I was a little afraid because I realized this was not a dream; it was real, but my real body was not with me. Then I saw a being of the greatest radiance, and the purest love seemed to flow from it. I do not know who it was, but I thought of the image that I have held of our Lord. It frightens me to even say that now," she said, her voice getting lower and softer.

"It is alright to say whatever you thought or felt or saw to me," replied Father Paolo.

"It did not speak, but somehow I knew that it gave me love and encouraged me to return to complete some mission and then I would come back. This place was so peaceful and free and full of love I didn't want to leave. Then suddenly, I felt you picking me up and I was glad I had come back," Janine said, never taking her eyes from his. "No one must know of this," she whispered fervently. "I will be thought to be a witch!"

"No one will know; it is your experience and it was given to you for a special reason. You are not the only one though to see this when near death. Two others have told me of similar experiences, one in the confessional and another on his deathbed. It is a very special gift and one to treasure. Is this why you have been troubled lately?" Father Paolo asked.

"No," she paused, "it has given me a great peace about death," she paused again, staring at the fireplace. "I have had thoughts about…uh…you." She looked up quickly into his clear blue eyes. "Since the night you took care of me and we prayed together, I have wanted to be with you more and I am struggling with myself and my commitment to God and also what you might think of my feelings. The turmoil inside is very painful," she said very softly as tears began to spill down her cheeks.

He slowly walked to the door, closed it, came back and knelt in front of her. "I have never known anyone like you. I never expected to meet anyone I would feel this way about. But I, like you, feel strongly about my promise to God. I feel neither of us is able, right now, to break that vow. There is nothing in the world that can change what we feel, but for now let us continue to pray for God's guidance and serve in the way we have chosen. For we are together here, Janine, and that is very precious to me," he said.

"To me also," she replied softly taking his hand. "Thank you, Fa . . . uh, Paolo, for helping me to find at least this much peace with the questions that have been tormenting me. I also feel this is what we must do. I am so happy that you feel the same as I do."

"It is time for the *nones* bell. For a hundred years, the bell has rung as ordered by Pope Callistes to remind all of the Turkish peril. Please go on down and I will join you in the refectory in a few minutes," he said softly as he rose to his feet. Holding her hands as she stood, he looked into her eyes and pressed her hands to his lips.

Chapter 11

Winter

Janine sat on the end of her cot, elbows on the windowsill, looking out over the snow covered meadows and the forested hills beyond. "If a day could be a color," she thought, "this one would be gray." The clouds were low and heavy.

It had been a busy season. She thought about the cheesemaking, and helping Mother Marguerite under Sister Clare's guidance. It had turned out beautiful and delicious and was stored with the cabbages in the cellar under the bell tower. The Christmas bell ringing would begin tomorrow morning and Father Paolo would involve some of the young lads from the village to ring the bell for an hour before the midnight mass on the eve of Christ's Day. Her thoughts drifted back to the day she and Father Paolo had gone into the forest with the cart and donkey to cut evergreen boughs of pine, fir and larch to decorate the church and refectory. "The evergreen is a symbol of immortality," he had said, "and Christ's birth gave us the hope of life eternal. As Isaiah said, 'To beautify the place of my sanctuary.'"

He had spoken of many of the events and customs of Christmas in other countries. In centuries past, he had said, before St. Boniface and other monks had come into East Franks and Gaul, the festival of Yule was celebrated honoring a triad of mother earth goddesses. It was the time of the yearly slaughter of livestock since there was inadequate feed over the winter with the pastures closed by snow. Many of the customs were impossible to stamp out with the coming of Christianity so they were absorbed into the festivals of the Church. In the early years, Christianity itself had been forced to adapt to the predominant religion of each area. The Roman Emperor Aurelius had built the Great Temple of the Sun and each year the greatest celebration was Brumalea when the sun began to rise again with renewed power - a week of festivities, eating, drinking, dancing and singing which culminated in *Kalends*, the beginning of a new year. The Christians celebrated the birth of their Savior at this time because the rulers would not have allowed them a separate holy day.

In the fourth century, the Bishop of Myra, a very wealthy man, who became known as St. Nicholas, secretly gave monies to all those in need that he could. Yes, the message that the Lord brought had touched many lives in the years that followed His death. There had been many beautiful hymns of adoration inspired by the birth of Jesus. St. Ambrose had written some and St. Francis, of course, had given *"Psalmas in Nativitate."* *"In excelsis gloria!"* Father Paolo had burst into song, and then went on to speak on his favorite subject: St. Francis. She smiled as she remembered.

The *Saint* had been the first to re-enact the manger, complete with a donkey, sheep and cow. This scene lingered in the minds of all the brothers and a new appreciation for the reality of the Babe spread. Father Paolo quoted Saint Luke, "And suddenly there was with the angel, a multitude of the heavenly host, praising God and saying, 'Glory to God in the highest and on earth, peace, good will toward men.'" He had asked her who she thought this 'multitude of heavenly host' was. She had pondered that before but had no answer and shook her head. "More angels, perhaps?" She wondered what his thoughts were on this 'heavenly host.'

Her thoughts were distracted a few minutes as she watched a fox slip quietly among the birch trees at the edge of the meadow. It was so fluffy and beautiful this time of year. They had seen several hares and even a red roe deer while they walked in the forest.

64

Paolo had talked of the hardships of the time when Christ was on earth. Herod was the tetrarch of Galilee, in the fifteenth year of the reign of Tiberius Caesar. When the wise men from the lands toward the rising sun came to find the one whose star they had followed for many months, they inquired of King Herod. He was one who took no chances of having his power diminished. In his life, he had drowned one brother-in-law, killed another, along with an uncle, his wife, his wife's mother and three of his sons. He had his own firstborn son, Antipater, executed five days before his own death. He had many spies and forbade any meetings. Bethlehem was not the only town to feel his wrath. In the city of Hyrcania overlooking the Dead Sea, many were executed. The Day of the Holy Innocents, which was three days after *Festum Navitates Domini Nostri Jesu Christi*, remembered these young babes who were killed by King Herod's orders trying to kill the new 'king'. So, the Church had perpetuated this celebration many centuries. In the tenth century, King Hakon had brought Christ's mass to the Norse people. And about the same time, an Arabian geographer, Georg Jacob, wrote the legend of the trees that bloomed and bore fruit at Christ's birth, despite the snow and ice.

Father Paolo was now in the village reminding each family of the custom begun by St. Francis to give extra corn and hay to their animals that they also might feel the love of the season. For St. Francis said, "If I could see the Emperor, I would implore him to have the people to throw corn and grain upon the byways so the birds might have enough to eat, especially our sisters, the larks." "The gentleness of that man!" she thought. "And the Savior whose life he had tried to imitate; they are so different from some men today who wage war and kill because they disagree on how to worship this Jesus. John Calvin was exiled in Geneva in Helvatia but many of those teaching his views were in all parts of France. The queen-mother, Catherine, had tried to affect a compromise but was not successful."

"These are not my concerns," Janine thought. She had seen none of these disbelievers. The churches and monasteries had, in almost all the wars, been spared destruction. She thought of the peace that came to her in trusting her life to God. Even now, she felt an ease spreading throughout her being. Thoughts of that day in the forest with Paolo infused that peace with joy.

The Bishop Perpetuus of Tours had begun the custom of fasting three days a week from *Novembre* 11 to Christ's mass in the year 490 and this had been decreased by only one day in all those years since. The two days of fasting each week this season had given her an unusual peace and clarity in her thoughts, she concluded as she opened the door to go down to vespers. The sweet scent of rosemary caught her attention. She was glad she had been able to grow it in abundance this past summer. The dried sprigs adorned the refectory with the evergreens. After the holy season, she would grind the rosemary and place bags of it under each person's *materas* to keep it fresh.

The Advent was indeed a 'coming' and the Nadal was near. It would be celebrated everywhere by almost everyone, she thought happily.

Chapter 12

Late Winter

"I sometimes feel very ineffective when I think of our beloved St. Francis: a small man, usually barefoot, and his great love as he went everywhere trying to tell everyone he met of the love of our Lord," said Father Paolo as they walked down the hill to the village.

"Yes," replied Janine, "He always said, 'God loves us all.' And his followers were always joyous. I understand they were called *joculatores* in their country. That area to the north of Rome in Umbria was very fortunate."

"It had its wars though," said Paolo. "When Francis was almost twenty years old, he joined the fighting between Assisi and Perugia to the north. As you know, he was captured by Perugia and imprisoned for over a year. It was after this that he renounced his family ties and all possessions and began to live on alms or working only for that day's food, and preaching Christ's words. As others began to join him, he required them to give up all possessions and he sent them by twos, one walking behind the other, to help the poor, the sick and the lepers. He wanted their lives to be the closest imitation of Christ's life possible. He felt the only necessary guide to perfect human existence was Christ's own life, but he upheld each person's concept of what they saw as spiritual perfection. This is the part of the saint's philosophy that may have been overlooked in the years that have come since his death," said Father Paolo. "Well, here we are."

"Good morning, Father Paolo, Sister Janine."

"*Pace a bene,*" replied Father Paolo as a young woman with babe in arms opened the door. "We heard you have not had milk for the little one Sybille, so we have brought some from our *Madame Roquefort.* May I?" he gestured to the baby as he handed her the ceramic jug. She exchanged the baby for the milk and they all went inside. Sybille took the jug that Janine carried also and smiled as they admired the smiling baby. Janine noticed the ease and love with which he held the little one. She had never seen one cry in his arms; they seemed to perceive his love.

"Is Jacques still cutting oak?" he asked.

"Yes," replied Sybille, "They are to begin loading tomorrow on the carts if we do not get snow. It is hard to work in such cold, but we must deliver to the barrel maker when he has a need."

"Please tell Jacques that I will come and help with the loading," Father Paolo said as he carefully passed the baby to Janine. His eyes met hers briefly as the conversation continued.

"And I will bring milk every second day until your cow is giving again," said Sister Janine.

"Thank you, both, and I have not forgotten your help in bringing my little one into the world," she said as Janine settled the babe in the mother's arms again.

"Peace and love," the priest entreated as they left the house.

"A beautiful baby," he said as they began the walk back up the hill toward the church.

"Yes indeed. Do you remember the child that Christ took in his arms and then said to His apostles, 'Whosoever shall receive one of such children in my name, receives me, and whosoever receives me, receives Him that sent me?'"

"Yes, a beautiful picture. Do you miss the orphanage, Janine?" he asked.

"I sometimes miss the children. There were times when I did not agree with their treatment, but there were so many. I did not have enough time to give as much as I wanted to each and every one," she replied.

"'Unless you become as little children'" quoted Paolo. "Are we as little children?" he asked. "Are we innocent, joyous each day, forgiving, spontaneous, trusting?"

Janine smiled at his introspection. "Who has bought that long-empty *chateaû* far down the valley that we can see from here?" she asked as she stopped and pointed toward the south.

"No one seems to know, only that several men live there and have several horses. Perhaps they will tend the vineyards; those have been neglected for a long time. I will call on them soon and extend our welcome," he replied.

Chapter 13

Early Spring

"Why has the schooling not begun? You were sent here with that mission and the Sister from St. Leonard was to be trained to help," the Bishop demanded loudly.

"I could see the people had to be able to feed their children before there would be any interest in educating them," Paolo responded. "This community was stricken. With the gristmill and further land clearing and some dikes on the river, several of the poorer families are now at least gaining, but not prospering. There is much to be done yet, but we are nearing the time when the school can begin. I have been teaching Sister Janine in church history and we are still gaining the confidence of the people. Apparently there were problems with Father Tomás."

The Bishop shrugged, "There have been questions about what is being taught to the Sister." His eyebrows reflected a question.

"As I have said - church history, teachings of Christ and, of course, general history for understanding our times," Father Paolo replied.

"Your learning in Toulouse and at university went far beyond the approved books. And this, as you know, is not to be promulgated by you," said the Bishop, peering at him intently.

"Yes, Your Excellency, I am very cognizant of the approved teachings," replied the friar.

"And do you not approve of that list?" questioned the Bishop loudly.

Father Paolo stared at the floor. "The list changes with the Councils," he said slowly. "I obey the holy fathers."

The Bishop gazed at him without speaking a few minutes, and then said, "There are many serious problems and attacks being waged upon our Holy Church, but I will not overlook the smallest heresy in one of my parishes, though the Calvinists burn our abbeys and the armies of Suleyman increase with each morning's sun." His voice had reached a near shout.

Quietly Father Paolo said, "I've heard that these two foes speak of each other; that the Emperor Suleyman asked concerning Martin Luther, 'How old is he? Forty-eight? I wish he were younger, he would find me a gracious protector.' And it is said that Luther replied, 'May God protect me from such a gracious protector!'"

Paolo smiled and then went on, "Luther urged the princes to back Emperor Charles against Suleyman and now the Emperor is dead; who is to stop the foe? The Emperor's sons cannot. Suleyman has ravaged Austria and King Louis of Hungary is gone, thrown from his horse in the battle, I hear, and drowned in a small stream, unable to move in his heavy armor. Emperor Charles was defeated in Algiers, with our King Francis allying himself with Suleyman to take Nice. When Emperor Charles defeated our King at Pavia near Milan and imprisoned him, our King appealed to Suleyman. Now our King Francis is gone too and Suleyman lives on. I have heard that he executed his son, Mustafa, eight years ago. His other son, Bayazid, sought refuge with the Shah and was held hostage. After he was released, Suleyman had him executed. His fleet even wintered at our own *La Cote d' Azur*."

"Yes, such an ally our king chose, just to have aid in trying to overcome Italy," said the Bishop sadly. "Those Islam devils are never converted. Their goal is to unite the world under Quranic law; ours is to bring the world to Christ. Oh, they 'allow' Christians to discreetly practice their religion, but a tax is levied upon them that is not placed on the Muslims in their empire. And he is named after Solomon! Ha!"

Father Paolo was relieved to find a topic upon which they agreed and that the inquisition to which he was being subjected had ceased. So he continued the discussion of the Turkish emperor, "Selim, Suleyman's father, slew *his* own father, two of his brothers and many other relatives, so it is said. They seem to be a rather ruthless people."

"He had over 100,000 men when he besieged the city of Rhodes, to gain entry into Egypt. And he was only twenty-eight years old at the time," replied the Bishop. "Their methods of warfare are diabolic. The *delils* are cloaked in leopard skins; the scouts and bowmen leave a trail of terror and burning villages for the cavalry armed with spears and swords. Next come the Janissaries in their towering headgear, armed with muskets and in the center is the Emperor in a white turban and bejeweled robe on a black horse accompanied by the band of drums, cymbals and *shawms*." He shook his head again.

"However, to discuss Suleyman and warfare was not my reason for coming all this way in this dreadful weather and risking attack on these back roads!" The Bishop started in anew. "I was hesitant to commission a Franciscan to this task, but with your background and certain 'commendations' you could be a successor to the Bishop in Toulouse with your holdings there." The Bishop eyed him quizzically.

Father Paolo shrugged, "My mother has an overseer of her properties. My life is committed to His work," he said lifting his eyes heavenward.

"God's work is accomplished in a myriad of ways, sometimes with our wealth, sometimes by the sword," debated the Bishop.

Father Paolo said nothing, just stared at the floor. His thoughts pondered the numbers who had died in the spreading of the message of love. It was the Council of Lyon in 1275 that gave the Franciscan Order ownership of all property in its use. This caused the Spirituals to request to leave the order and remain wandering preachers. They were called Fraticelli in Italy and put to the Inquisition! "I see you do not wish to discuss your lands in the shadow of the Pyrenees. Very well, our Holy Father Pius IV does not require you to give up lands, though Pope John condemned the Franciscan vow of poverty many years ago," countered the Bishop.

"I have no properties. My mother handles her possessions," Father Paolo replied.

"You have made two trips in the past three years to the south," the Bishop continued, "Was that not to deal with urgent business? You realize there is a tax on your income from there, do you not?"

"I have no income from there. An illness of my mother, who asked for me, took me to Toulouse," Paolo replied. "I do not wish to go back to Toulouse simply because the family holdings would interfere and make more difficult the keeping of the vows I have taken."

"And your vow of chastity?" queried the Bishop.

"I keep all my vows, each as faithfully as the other," he replied with set jaw, meeting the Bishop's eyes unwaveringly.

"Well, we have serious abuses of Holy Law. There are some clerics who do not even know Holy Law; they rush and mumble through the masses, neglect the fast, and many are not celibate!" shouted the Bishop.

"The practice of some abbots holding more than one benefice and offices given 'in commendam' as a reward for services to the Pope have impoverished many abbeys," said Paolo, realizing that he was treading on very dangerous ground.

The Bishop's face reddened; he retorted, "Not in my area is it allowed! Have you forgotten Ludovico Barbo, appointed commendatory abbot of St. Guistina at Padua by Pope Gregory in 1408? He took the habit and reformed the abbey. Holy Father Eugenius gave them a special rule that placed much emphasis on meditation and prayer."

"Yes, I've always found that story inspiring. But the 'Concordat of 1516' has allowed many of the abbotships to be filled by the kings, and it is used freely; some offices are even sold, I have heard," replied Father Paolo.

"That is hearsay! I'm surprised that you mention it," smirked the Bishop. "The kings have not liked the fact that our Holy Father, the Pope, rules the people and therefore, rules the countries, but there have been many 'cooperations.' For example, in 1233 the Pope entrusted the combating of heresies to local agencies of the King."

"But this took away the control he had over the inquisitorial methods," replied Paolo. "Then in 1334, King Louis proclaimed Pope John a heretic, saying, 'You are as if under the dominion of those grasses that produce visions. The weaknesses of the wicked are the same as the weaknesses of the saintly.'"

"Recently," said the Bishop, "Henry the Eighth in England rejected the Holy Law so he could 'put away' his wife for another, and, of course, the Huguenots are encouraged by his turning against the Church. And now that England has many ships and has begun venturing the oceans their minister said, 'The Pope has no right to partition the world and give kingdoms to whomever he pleases.' There will be more wars over these explorations, mark my words. Already the Castilians sail to the new lands. The Portuguese are granted all new lands and islands south of Cape Bojador."

"Yes, my brother, who is also a friar, has sailed with a fleet of Castilian explorers across the ocean. They have not returned," replied Paolo.

"I did not know you had a brother," said the Bishop.

"Yes, he is younger than me by five years," replied Paolo.

"So, he travels with the Castilians?" asked the Bishop.

"Yes, he was schooled in Barcelona and the Basque Provinces," replied Paolo.

"So, he went to the south and did not follow in your steps to Paris?" responded the Bishop.

"We have both always been intrigued by new places, from our father, I suppose, who traveled widely in his business and frequently took us with him," said Paolo.

"And what business was that?" asked the Bishop.

"Oh, just the usual buying and selling," replied Paolo noncommittally. "Oh, I have neglected the hour and see it is time for the vespers bell. Will you lead our office?" asked Paolo.

"Well, of course!" snorted the Bishop.

"Our repast will be an hour after prayers. I'm sure Mother Marguerite has planned something wonderful in your honor," said the friar.

⁓∋

Janine noticed Paolo did not seem his usual joyous self. The Bishop sat at the head of the long table, and she wondered how he ate so heartily with the encumbrance of his heavily brocaded robes. They seemed so stiff. She looked at the soft beige homespun habits of the others and felt a sense of comfort. The coachers were not allowed at the table, but ate in the kitchen and she could hear their coarser talk and suppressed laughter at times.

The Bishop was discoursing, between bites, on the state of the world; how the English had by vote of clergy, under duress, transferred all rights and duties of the Pope to their King. Bishop Fisher and Sir Thomas More had refused to swear to this Act of Supremacy and were beheaded. She had heard all this since it was nearly thirty years past - before her birth, in fact. So, her thoughts wandered as she halfway listened. She wondered what had precipitated this unannounced visit of their Bishop.

Now, he was expounding on their country's good fortune that the English had been expelled from French soil before this disease of insurrection and heresy began. Helvatia and the Low Countries were completely overrun with these new ideas. "'Scripture is the sole source of revelation,' says Luther," the Bishop quoted. "Ha! They even reject the primacy of the Holy See and deny the necessity of sacrament! They trust only in God's guidance; how can they ascertain guidance when that comes only through the Holy Church and her priests?" his voice had reached a fevered pitch. He turned to Father Paolo, who seemed to have withdrawn inside his own thoughts. She knew how his simple trust in God was offended by these kinds of tirades.

Father Paolo replied, "Well, King Henry's edict of *Ecouin* two years ago has not slowed the spread of this philosophy."

"Philosophy!!? Ha!" the Bishop retorted loudly. "Heresy it is! The Queen mother and her chancellor *Michel de L'Hospital* called us together last year at Orleans to try to come to a peaceful compromise. We cannot compromise the beliefs of our Holy Church!" His voice rose again. "But she is urging toleration, while these 'churches' spring up like the plague. The noble house of *duc de Guise* will not allow this! He has many strong followers and I suspect an army is forming. The Huguenots were given liberty of conscience a year ago and now they want liberty of worship! In Lyon, the poorer people are flocking to these orators of Calvin. That is one reason I am here. It is rumored that a Protestant group called *des Adrets* is forming in this area or to the south. Have you heard of this group, Father Paolo?" asked the Bishop.

"No, as far as I know, there are none sympathetic to these ideas here in our village. I heard rumors when I was last in Toulouse, but no talk of revolt," replied Paolo.

"I have heard that these Protestants have hired outsiders, Landsknechts from Bavaria and warmongers and mercenaries from Helvatia and even Italy. Everyone must get involved! And our country is once again embroiled in bloodshed," the Bishop went on.

Janine was amazed at the amount of food the Bishop managed to put away while expounding his 'news.' Sister Jacqueline seemed preoccupied. It appeared Mother Marguerite had closed her hearing of the continuing upsetting monologue. Janine turned her head slightly toward the door, for she thought she heard a faint knock through the ongoing emotional tirade at the other end of the table. She quietly slipped away to the side door and opened it noiselessly. There, in the light spilling out the doorway, were two lepers, a man and, apparently, his wife. The man said, "Could we find shelter from this cold rain and snow in the hay in your stable and beg of you some food to carry us through?"

"Of course," said Janine, "come into the kitchen."

"My children," said Father Paolo, coming up behind her, "please, come in by the fire. Why, your sores are in need of tending. You will not stay in the stable. We have room here. I'm sure the Bishop is sorrowed at your discomfort and will want you to stay in our *dormitorie*." He glanced at the Bishop who seemed to be sputtering, at a loss for words for once. "Sister Jacqueline, please put the large kettles on the fire. Sister Clare, have you some very soft cloths?" Paolo asked.

"Of course, Father Paolo," said Clare as she hobbled off to her cell by the kitchen. The lepers seemed terrified at so much attention and shrank back against the closed door. Janine led them gently toward the kitchen.

"Coachers!" screamed the Bishop, and they sprang from the kitchen almost colliding with the lepers. They veered away sharply with looks of fear and repulsion on their faces.

"Father Paolo, this is most unusual," said the Bishop.

"Like our revered St. Francis, we tend the sick and homeless here, your Lordship," replied Father Paolo.

"Franciscans!" the Bishop said under his breath. "You will actually tend their sores? You will be next to the leprosarium," predicted the Bishop.

"Sister Janine and I will care for them. God's will be done. He cares for us," replied the priest.

"I must go back to Lyon," said the Bishop abruptly.

"*Tonight*, Your Excellency? In this weather?" asked Paolo.

"Yes, but our conversation is not finished," he said curtly. "The Abbot at *Clermont-Ferrand* and a council will want to question *you* further concerning your 'teaching.' I want you and Sister Janine to come to *Lyon* by *Palme Dimanche*," ordered the Bishop.

"But, Your Honor, my flock, at Paschaltide? And we have only the donkey and cart," entreated Paolo.

"I will send my coach and Father Tomás," replied the Bishop.

"Father Tomás?" questioned Paolo.

"Yes, he will most likely want to visit his former flock," said the Bishop.

"Of course, Your Excellency," said Paolo with a blank expression but tight jaw.

"Coachers! Where are your torches? Make the horses ready!" demanded the Bishop. They looked at him aghast.

"Go!" he ordered and they scurried out grumbling among themselves.

Janine could see from the kitchen the torches being lit. The mud and ice, she knew, was ankle deep by the stables. Senór Siquenza, Father Paolo's donkey, was braying at the commotion near his stall. Father Paolo had escorted the Bishop to his room to gather his belongings and then gone out with a torch to see if he could help the coachers while Janine prepared food for the lepers and peeked out from time to time. Sister Jacqueline had disappeared. "As usual," Janine thought.

Two of the horses seemed to have revolted at this idea and had broken away. Two of the coachers were chasing them with torches, which seemed to frighten the horses even more. One jumped the low stonewall and headed toward the village. One coacher was swearing many curses on the animal as he tried to run in the icy mud. Janine had not seen such confusion and chaos since the night of the fire at the orphanage.

Eventually, Father Paolo came back to the refectory, thoroughly soaked. The coachers seemed to be getting all the horses together and were gathering harnesses. The Bishop shuffled into the refectory, looking at Father Paolo's disarray with a sniff.

"Bring the nun; there will be questions," he ordered.

Sister Jacqueline rushed into the refectory in a cape that was damp with rain spots carrying a sturdy cloth pouch.

"Your Excellency," she said breathlessly, "I am ready. You promised to take me with you."

"I don't know what you are speaking of," the Bishop said curtly.

"The letters; you said you would arrange for me to go back to Dijon near my home. I did what you asked," Jacqueline pleaded and fell to her knees clutching at his hand. Janine had come to the doorway of the kitchen and she and Paolo looked on with quizzical interest.

"Get up, Sister! I don't know what you're speaking of, but you may go to *Lyon* and we will see to your placement," said the Bishop. As she rose, one side of the pouch fell open and gold francs spilled out. Janine recognized the pouch as being the one she had seen in the cellar. Paolo knelt to help her retrieve the coins.

"What is this, Sister Jacqueline?" he asked knowingly.

"It is mine!" she barked.

"Is it an inheritance?" he quizzed. "Or has your weekly shopping been more than you could handle?"

"It is mine," she repeated and looked threateningly at the Bishop.

"I'm sure she is taking her . . . ah . . . inheritance to give to the poor in *Lyon*," intercepted the Bishop.

"Uh huh," said Paolo, staring at her until she defiantly walked out into the rain, her head held high.

The Bishop followed, shouting at the coachers to bring the carriage up. After the clatter of horses and coach on the cloister had died away, Paolo came in shaking his head sadly. He looked at Janine, still standing by the doorway. Their eyes met in acknowledgment of what had been happening. They both just smiled sadly and proceeded to get water and cloths ready for caring for their special guests.

Chapter 14

Late Spring

"Why are the Muhammedans so hated?" Janine asked as the coach sent by the Bishop bounced along over muddy roads.

"Mostly because they deny that our Lord is the Son of God. They speak of Jesus as a prophet. The Church speaks of Mohammed as an imposter, possessed by the devil and his words, a deliberate falsification. And yet, there are some interesting stories about the Muslims. About 400 years ago, the abbot of Cluny, who was also called Peter the Venerable, visited Espania, which was held by the Arabs at that time. He found a prosperous culture with innovative irrigating systems, highly advanced studies of medicine, many new inventions and libraries of immense size. In Cordoba alone, there were seven hundred mosques and the streets were paved with stones and bricks. It is said the Great Library in Alcazar was the greatest in the world at that time. It was destroyed in one of their internal conflicts but the many books were sent to other cities. Even prior to this, the area, then called Al-Andulus, was producing silk, wool, glass, brass, pottery, gold, silver and swords. The Arabs were regularly delivering letters from that part of their empire to the east as far as India. The Muslims had been in Castile about three hundred years, calling it the land of the Vandals."

"At any rate, the abbot commissioned the first translation of their Qur'an into Latin so there have been Qur'anic studies at

Cluny for some time. An Arabic text of that Scripture was published in Venice around the time of my birth and the Pope ordered it burned. The Council of Florence in 1442 declared, 'outside the Catholic Church, no one will have a share in eternal life,' also indicating that there were no prophets outside those recognized by the Church."

"Yes, I have heard that quote many times," replied Janine. "But have you read these translations? What do they teach?"

"Yes, I've read the Qur'an, when I was quite young and had private teachers. One was from the city of Cordoba and he had many books not available in Toulouse at that time. The Qur'an speaks of Abraham as the first believer in One God. The Arabs are said to be descendants of Ishmael, Abraham's son by Hagar. Muhammed spoke of himself as a messenger bringing again the primeval truths of God, saying, 'to me it has been revealed that your God is One God.' He spoke also of Noah, Moses, David, Solomon and Jesus. He claimed the spiritual messenger in his ecstatic visions was the Angel Gabriel. The basic tenets of Islam, which means 'submission,' are prayer, five times a day, a month a year of fasting, the giving of alms, profession of their faith, and the pilgrimage to Mecca. Their prayer is their worship. Their fasting is from dawn to sundown and includes *sexuel abstinence*." Paolo glanced at Janine briefly. She only nodded her understanding with no expression.

He went on, "Their creed may be seen in one of their *suras*: 'He is God, One God, the Everlasting Refuge, who has not begotten and has not been begotten and equal to Him is not anyone.' So the miraculous conception is completely rejected by them."

"I see," said Janine. "Castile is no longer under Arab control. What happened to the Arabs?" she asked.

"They were expelled from the country along with the Jews almost a hundred years ago when the Kingdom of Granada fell. Alfonso the Sixth was able to reunite the three Christian kingdoms of Leon, Castile and Galicia around the middle of the eleventh century. They chose Rodrigo Diaz de Vibar as commander of their armies. He was called El Cid or Sidi, which meant Lord.

The Holy Father in Rome had given his blessing to this conquest and El Cid was described as the perfect Christian knight, chivalrous and gentle. Those 'evil' Arabs had never seen such a barbarian! It was said in stories handed down from Castile that he used every atrocity, raped, pillaged and plundered. They pushed south to Toledo below Madrid on the Tagus River. The library they found in Toledo was a treasure to scholars everywhere. This city had been the Visigoth capitol for 200 years before the Arab invasion of 711. It was another 400 years before the Arabs were expelled from power, but this was the beginning.

"Is it true that they have many wives?" asked Janine.

"Yes, they are sometimes called concubines, as in the days of Abraham. I've heard some powerful Arabs have so many that they must have eunuchs to watch over them. Their law forbids emasculating other Muslims so they choose either African or Christian men living in their area. A concubine that displeases her master is sewn into a weighted sack and dropped into the sea!" said Paolo looking at her seriously.

"A good reason not to be a Muhammedan," said Janine. They both laughed.

"Emperor Suleyman calls himself 'Protector of the Holy Cities of Medina, Mecca and Jerusalem' but he rules from Constantinople. Did you know in the Arabic language there is no word for conscience?" asked Paolo.

"They have no concept of this?" she asked.

"That's what I've been told. Also, I have heard that their city of Jiddeh in Arabic is called *Ummuna Hawa*, which means Our Mother, Eve. Isn't that interesting?"

Janine nodded slowly, realizing the implication.

"They have no priesthood, only scholars of the Qur'an called 'ulama,'" Paolo continued. Yes, this merchant who claimed to be a descendent of Abraham, as the Jews, is most interesting.

"Guilbert of Nogent spoke of Muhammad in his *Gesta Dei* saying, 'It doesn't make any difference if we speak ill of someone whose wickedness exceeds all measure anyway.' The hatred goes back many hundred of years, even before the Crusades. In 1187 when the Sultan Saladin conquered Jerusalem, the cross of our Lord was never seen again. It is fortunate that a piece had been brought to Rome in the fourth century," said Paolo.

"Why can't everyone just worship God and be peaceful?" asked Janine. Father Paolo just shook his head.

"Are you warm?" he asked, tucking the woolen *couvre-lit* around her feet.

"I am fine, thank you, Father Paolo," she replied with a warm smile.

"I am sorry this journey was demanded. I'm afraid my pursuit of knowledge and my heritage in the Languedoc have kept the Bishop's eye on me," said Paolo, his eyes downcast.

"I am not sorry. I never even dared envision having a journey with you," she replied staring at him earnestly. To break the spell of their eyes, she looked out the open window of the coach and quickly went on, "I see the soil here is black, very unlike the red soil of St. Leonard and Aubusson. They grow beautiful cabbages there.

"Yes," he said, "but this is quite fertile. *Le Puy*, where we will stay overnight at the abbey, is in an unusual setting. It has three large rocky outcroppings of this rough black stone. The Cathedral of Notre Dame is on the south slope of one of these, and the sacristy there has a Bible that is inscribed on purple parchment, said to be over five hundred years old. We will say prayers there so we can see it before continuing our journey tomorrow."

They rode in silence for quite some time each with their own thoughts. Suddenly, Father Paolo quoted, "'And Enoch walked with God; and he was not; for God took him.' He was three hundred sixty-five years old when he went with God or as our St. Paul said, 'By faith, Enoch was taken away without dying and he was seen no more because God took him.' Do you understand that?" he asked.

"No," she replied, "But I accept it. His son, Methuselah, so it is written, lived 969 years. The oldest person I have known lived to be sixty-one. I don't understand that either."

"Has no one since Enoch pleased God?" Paolo questioned. Janine shrugged her shoulders. "Why was he so special?" he asked.

"We believe death is our fate or release. Perhaps he was not concerned about death like we are. You are again asking very difficult questions, Paolo," Janine replied softly.

"The question troubles me," he replied seriously.

"Now I must quote," said Janine smiling. "'Let not your heart be troubled. Peace I leave with you, my peace I give to you.'"

He smiled. "Your trust in God strengthens me." Their eyes met in the fading light. The long shadows were giving way to a cold twilight as the coach bounced along.

The next morning was cool, but the clouds had gone overnight and the sun was brilliant. The coach climbed up steep wooded hills and rumbled down into valleys dotted with farms. Brown stone houses built with much mortar, the hayricks, the walnut trees, and fields bordered by low stonewalls gave a pastoral scene of serenity. As they came nearer the Rhone Valley, vineyards were more common. They passed wine drawers slowly making their way north with the season like the swallows. Janine noticed some towns had goldsmiths and tilemakers. This *luxe* was very different from *Villefranche* where the struggle was obvious. She wondered if Paolo's thoughts were on his flock there or on the upcoming meeting with the Bishop in Lyon as he gazed out the open window of the coach door.

She found that she was wrong on either guess as he suddenly quoted, "'So Moses stayed there with the Lord for forty days and forty nights, without eating any food or drinking any water and he wrote on the tablets the words of the covenant, the ten commandments. As Moses came down from Mount Sinai with the two tablets of the commandments in his hands, he did not know that the skin of his face had become radiant while he conversed with the Lord.'" He paused. "The Israelites were afraid to come near him, so after he had finished speaking with them, he put a veil over his face and wore it except when he went into the meeting place. A cloudy pillar descended and stood at the door of the tent when Moses conversed with God." He turned from staring out the window. "I wonder just how Moses appeared that the people were so afraid."

"You dwell on the most mystical passages, Father Paolo," Janine replied. "To see even the passing of God much less converse with Him would be the greatest experience one could possibly have."

"Yes, we find that experience no where else. When Jesus spoke to St. Paul on the road to Damascus, he was blinded for three days," replied Paolo.

Janine smiled marveling at the complexity of this man. He looked at her curiously and smiled back, saying, "What a beautiful day! This is the day the Lord has made! What are your thoughts?"

Janine recognized his use of the quote usually given on Easter morning. "I was thinking that Sister Clare is filled with new energy since our new Sister Mary has come to learn from her," she said.

"Yes, though she is very young, Sister Mary seems to have a gift with the weaving. Mother Marguerite had heard of her and arranged for her transfer to us. She is from Aubusson not far from your orphanage and apparently has a family background of weaving," said Paolo. "Your love and care have made Sister Clare's affliction easier. The daily baths with herbs that you help her into seem to ease her pain some."

"She is a beautiful one and Sister Mary will learn much more than weaving from her," predicted Janine.

"Perhaps with training she can also help us with teaching," said Paolo. "Do you feel ready to begin that mission this *automne*?

"I'm not sure I am ready; but our village is growing and we have quite a number of children," Janine replied. "You were taught at home by private teachers?"

"Yes, mostly. Our chateau was in a somewhat remote area overlooking the Garonne River," he replied.

"Your father was very wealthy?" Janine asked.

"Well, yes, and my mother was the only heir to a large estate in the Basque provinces as well."

"Your mother is Castilian?" she asked.

"Yes, she is very beautiful with dark eyes and hair. She is distantly related to the *Viscount of Castilbo* whose daughter married the Count of Foix and formed the sovereignty of Andorra. Ah, the Pyrenees are beautiful," he reflected with a far away look in his eyes. "There is snow in some places year round. On one mountain side there is a huge amphitheatre carved by the forces of nature. The waterfalls plunging down the sides must be the highest in the world. Of course, I've not seen *all* the world!" he laughed.

"The great Ebro River has its beginnings there as well as several of our own rivers. There are beautiful little cushions of tiny flowers and little deer are occasionally seen there. The shepherds in these mountains must be very rugged. High in the mountains above Lourdes, the sulfur springs have drawn ailing people since the time of our Lord."

"Toulouse," Paolo went on, "also has its beauty - the hills are full of orchards and even the chalky highlands with their straggling oaks have their charm. The villages are built against the cliffs to conserve the valuable fields. Many of the towns are fortified *bastildes*, due to the wars that have raged back and forth. The chateau at *Monségur* was the scene of one of the last sieges in the crusade against the Cathar heresy. Two hundred Cathari were burned at the stake. At Albi, the Cathedral of Sainte-Cecil is fortified and served as the center of the Inquisition of that heresy. Of course, this Inquisition turned families and neighbors against each other. The nobility of the area had encouraged this new theology for there was at that time some conflict with the

Holy Fathers in Rome, but this leniency met with ruthless cruelty. The entire town of Beziers was destroyed; the lands were seized by the crusaders. I have heard that there is a huge cave in the Pyrenees where six hundred people were walled up and starved to death, but that was in 1238 and, I think, not connected with the Inquisition," he paused.

"My father's ancestors have long been in Languedoc so I know of its troubles and its beauties."

"You miss it, I can tell," said Janine.

"Yes, at times, but I am nearer than I've been in many years. And I have a mission and a vow," he replied. "The Bishop wants me to go to Toulouse and has indicated that he will arrange a benefice for me if I will accept my place as an heir in that community. That is, of course, if I am not found to be a heretic in these questionings!" He laughed heartily and then turned to her seriously, "I may be sent to Montpelier or Toulouse as an instructor at one of the universities, for the Bishop knows of my Franciscan vows. Would I see you ever again? Will we ever feel differently about our vows? If we did, what could we do?"

"Father Paolo!" Janine interrupted. "None of these things have happened. Let us not use our strength on them. These questions have occurred to me also and I know that I want to be near you and perhaps an answer will present itself at that time. For now, let us trust our conferences will go well."

Father Paolo bowed his head and said softly, "Yes, yes, I am too independent in my thoughts to have taken vows. Several tried to tell me that."

"Paolo," she interrupted again softly, taking his hands in hers, "you are a wonderful priest, full of love and energy and wisdom. Do not . ."

Suddenly the carriage lurched forward as the coachers yelled at the horses and cracked the whips. Janine was thrown at Paolo's feet. The carriage rolled sideways, now going faster than ever, and Paolo was thrown into the floor on top of Janine. She struggled to right herself. "Stay down," he ordered. "There is some danger."

He attempted to crawl to the door, but the coach tilted again, throwing him beside her again. There were sounds of musket fire and Paolo realized that some enemy had recognized the Bishop's coach. It seemed the carriage might overturn any time. He threw his arm and cape over Janine and closed his eyes in a brief prayer.

❦

The boats of the water merchants were moving busily along the swollen Rhone. The sunny days had greatly increased its volume. Among the many goods offered were patterned carpets that had come from Turkistan, as well as silks from the Far East and frankincense from aromatic trees in Arabia. Cotton and indigo came in from Egypt. The bustle and noise of the city was in sharp contrast to the two strolling, mutely clad figures on the river front embankment boulevard.

"I see *Lyon* has followed the example of Paris in prohibiting the dumping of chamber pots into the paved streets," said the priest. "*Lyon, as* you know, was once an independent principality, ruled by the Archbishops. The Bishop would be in his glory if that were still true today! Paolo laughed. "Are you enjoying being here?" he asked.

"Yes, very much," replied Janine. "I have never seen anything like the Cathedral of St. John, and the *dimache des Rameaux*! The procession led by the Bishop carrying real palm leaves brought all the way from the mer, the boys' choir greeting the procession with 'Gloria, laus and honor,' the bells, the crowds and the 'Hosanna.' It is uplifting! Is that why we do all these things? To feel 'lifted' closer to God? Is God pleased?"

"Our ritual is not important to God. But the ritual leads us to our inner feelings, inner heart and our heart leads us to losing ourselves, our pride, our fears, and that leads us closer to God," replied Father Paolo. They walked slowly, both glad to be together again.

"There will be the washing of the feet by the priests and the Bishop tonight and the altar will be denuded. And in the ancient tradition, no bells will be tolled until 'He is risen,'" said Paolo. "Then, on the morrow will be the Pasch of Crucifixion and the adoration of the Cross."

"Has the Bishop had questions of you?" asked Janine.

"Yes, just in conversation. Our meeting with the abbot and archdeacon will be tomorrow. Why do you suppose that he insisted that I take this walk with you! I would venture that he is at one of those windows on the upper level. Have you ever seen a manor house like the Bishop's?"

"No," replied Janine, "the Bishop at Limoges had a lovely house, but not nearly as large as this. I think Irenaeus, bishop here at Lyon in the second century, could not have imagined anything like this. It was the Christians then, who were treated as heretics, by the Romans, brought to trial for not worshipping their gods and tortured to death for sport. Irenaeus' predecessor, Bishop Pothinius, died in prison of torture and exposure at a very old age. This happened while Irenaeus was in Rome bringing an account of what the Christians were suffering in Gaul."

"Very good!" praised Father Paolo. "You remember what we talked about last year and you've done your reading." Janine just smiled. "Have you enjoyed staying in the convent?" he asked.

"Yes, very much. Thank you for interceding when the Bishop offered lodging in his manor," said Janine.

"I though you might have missed the companionship of being with others of your order."

"It is a great inspiration to be with such large groups of Sisters in prayer and in choir," said Janine.

"Did I also detect your discomfort at the Bishop's dress and conversation?" asked Paolo.

"Chastity, poverty, humility and obedience we are taught and we live by. Obedience to His Serene Highness is one of my vows," she replied stiffly.

Father Paolo stared sideways at her, questioningly, a slight smile appearing.

"There are many things I do not understand; I try to leave them with God." Janine glanced at his smile. "I am not a trouble maker like you," she retorted impishly.

"It's good to see you smile," he said softly.

"Look! The violets and pennycress are coming through in the sheltered and sunny spots. Spring has come again! There is even a faint greening in some of the willows," Janine remarked.

"Nature is the daughter of God. The mountains to the east still have much snow though," he observed.

"Father Paolo, I have heard rumors of a war against the believers of Calvin," Janine stated questioningly.

"Yes, those following *Francois, duc de Guise*, swept upon a Protestant gathering at Vassy two weeks ago and massacred almost all, over 200 people. I have heard they are now taking control of the royal palace in Paris. What is the queen mother with a child king to do? Her attempt at compromise has failed. Her Edict of *Janviere* seems to bring war instead of the tolerance she intended. Well, we must turn back; it will soon be time for *nones* prayers and there will be no bells today," said Paolo.

"The *probléme* goes back to our King Henry. In siding with the Protestant princes against Emperor Charles of the Holy Roman Empire, he weakened our position as defenders of the Faith," argued the archdeacon.

"He had to stop the Emperor or he would have overrun our own country," countered the Prior. "The Peace of *Chateau-Cambrisis* took Savoy from him and gave it independence. Then Emperor Charles was crowned king of Italy by the Holy Father."

"But, the issue goes back further," interjected the Bishop, "Henry's father, Francis, was interested only in matters *Italienne* and filling the treasuries. Intoxicated by the writing of that

91

Machiavelli, his two-faced policy of attacking Calvinists here and supporting the Lutheran princes across the border was confusing to everyone. He pretended support of our Holy Father Clement while making an alliance with Henry the Eighth of England who was openly assuming all rights and duties of the Holy Father for himself in England! Yes, King Francis was decadent; consider the palace at Chambord!" His voice reached a booming pitch.

"Enormous towers, an overabundance of pinnacles," he continued, "built to impress the *Comtesse de Thoury* who lived nearby and who was the object of his youthful passion. Of course, the hunting on the sandy plains attracted him too. Décadence! Now see where it has brought us." He paused. "Come in, Father Paolo. We were just speaking of where the monarchs have taken us. You had a taste of the situation on your journey here. *Mon ami*, my carriage was chased and fired upon whilst coming with Father Paolo and the Sister. The coachers almost overturned in the chase."

Looks of shock were on each face, "Were either of you wounded?" asked the Prior.

"No, Your Honor, we were only bounced about. We soon came into civilized country and they gave up the chase," replied Father Paolo.

"So, you can see what we are dealing with here," said the Bishop. "I have heard there are almost two thousand of these groups meeting. Now we have a child king and this *Catherine de Medicis*. The Concordat in 1516 gave King Francis control over heresies, but the Inquisition was never exercised as in the Kingdom of Castile. Francis, instead, chose to set up two new chambers, three score of judges and, of course, he sold each of these offices. Then his son set up the *présidial* with sixty-five new courts and still nothing is done about heresy," the Bishop was into a fomentation by now.

Father Paolo's attention strayed to the room with its crackling fireplace, large sunny windows, beautiful tapestries and paintings. "One could study in comfort here," he thought.

"The Protestants are assembling forces at Orléans under *Prince de Condi* and *Admiral Gaspard de Coligny*, right now," said the archdeacon.

"This must not go out of this room," said the Bishop, looking around at Father Paolo and the others," the Cardinal of Lorraine and the Duke of Guise have a very strange man working secretly with them. His name is *Michel de Nostredame*. He is now the physician to the young king and his medical training is seemingly from Montpelier. It is said there may be an attempt to seize the throne," he said lowering his voice, so that everyone drew a little nearer. "This man has written some very bizarre works, but I don't believe there has been any official acceptance of them. The Duke of Guise, as you know, is married to Anne, Duchess of Gisors, with connections to the Gonzaga family and some speak of him as intolerant, brutal and bloodthirsty, but he defends our cause, regardless of what his motive may be."

"Is it true that the Lorraine family is of Jewish origin?" asked the archdeacon.

"The entire history of Gaul is intertwined with Israelite implications. The laws of the Teutonic tribes paralleled the laws of Israel. The tribe of Benjamin dispersed into Sparta and Arcadia and the Phoenician traders brought them to Narbonne and up the Rhone before the time of our Lord. Their descendants claimed a lineage back to ancient Troy and the Old Testament," said the Bishop. "It has been suggested that this lineage established the Order of Knights Templars. Pope Innocent protected them and they amassed a great deal of wealth. There was a lot of intrigue when Pope Benedict was killed and our King Phillip managed to have his Archbishop of Bordeaux elected as Clement the Fifth. Then, all the Templars were arrested in one night and put to the Inquisition. Their leader was roasted over a slow fire. It is curious, though; their *preceptory* near *Bézu* was not touched. It is said Pope Clement was related to the commander there. There were preposterous rumors then that these Templars protected the lineage of Christ! Of course, we all know that our Lord had no progeny! It is interesting though that Pope Clement and King Phillippe died in that same year after the siege."

The Bishop seemed lost in thought for a minute. "So, Father Paolo, what are your thoughts on all this?" asked the Bishop.

"I was just wondering what St. Francis would have said of it, Your Excellency," replied Paolo. "Perhaps, he would quote our Lord: "Blessed are the meek, for they shall inherit the earth . . . blessed are the merciful for they shall obtain mercy.""

"Father Paolo, one day you seem to be questioning the Holy Law and the next you are as humble as St. Francis himself!" sighed the Bishop. "I know not whether to recommend you as Bishop of Toulouse or charge you with impiety! I see qualities of strength that would be valuable, but your curiosity, obstinate nature and questioning worries me. Have you considered the certain privileges that might go with the position I have suggested? You could assign 'certain ones' to your area," he looked at him with a raised eyebrow then went on, "but as a friar, you have no control, you can only ask of others."

"I would like to establish the school for the villagers at *Villefranche* now, Your Excellency; perhaps I may feel differently about Toulouse at a later time," he replied.

"Franciscans! Pope John and Pope Boniface should have ousted the entire lot!" sputtered the Bishop.

The archdeacon and abbot looked slightly shocked, though they were used to the Bishop's outbursts. The archdeacon knew of the privileges of which he spoke. The Bishop's mistress was one of the most beautiful women he had ever seen.

"The *des Adrets* are gaining strength in the south. They will be encouraged to boldness by the armies at Orléans. You must send a messenger to me, Friar Paolo, if you detect an army in your area, and I will try to dispatch help," said the Bishop.

"Of course, Your Lordship," replied Paolo.

"Now, of other matters; there is talk of changing our calendar. The council recommends the old Roman tradition of *Kalends* and beginning our new year then instead of on *Paschaltide*, but for now our new year begins Sunday," related the Bishop.

"Please prepare yourselves for our vigil of prayer throughout the night tomorrow. I will have no sleeping as some were seen to do last year!" he snorted, looking at the archdeacon. "Resurrection service with communion will be after matins, as you know. What other concerns were we going to discuss, Deacon Raoul?"

"The conflict over Moses writings, Your Honor," said the archdeacon.

"Ah, yes, a certain Flemish gentleman, Andreas van Maes, has written a book stating that the death of Moses is written in the same style as the texts that precede it. His book has been placed on the Index of Prohibited Books. If you see copies, you must send them to the Holy Father in Rome. As you know, the Church contends that Moses wrote the entire Pentateuch. How this was done is left up to God. Even Tostatus, the bishop of Avila, stated that certain passages, such as those relating to Moses death could not have been written by Moses. I'm not sure why he was not excommunicated or at least called before the council. This same idea has come up before and it has always been rejected. Even a Jewish court physician spoke of it and was called a blunderer. As was once quoted of a Spanish rabbi, 'And he who understands will keep silent.'" The Bishop looked around the room at each silent face. Paolo's face was blank, but his inner thoughts were tumbling in turmoil. He had read all these works with great interest, not to discredit Moses, but to understand.

The Bishop was continuing about Holy Father Pius reconvening the Council of Trent and how King Henry had discouraged the Bishops from attending the previous council. He spoke of the founding of a new school by the new Order of Jesuits.

Paolo was thinking yet of Moses' work as the Bishop talked of some riots breaking out in the city because of the printing presses. Fewer laborers were needed so many had been left without work. Sometimes the concerns of the Bishop and the Holy

Father seemed so remote from the people of his village. He suddenly felt a great wave of love for those simple people.

~⊙

The light was streaming through the stained glass windows, softly bestowing itself upon the arcade and the chancel on the left side of the huge cathedral. The Poor Clares were all in a bay together and Father Paolo could see Janine in the glow. Her beauty captured him completely. He wondered what the abbess had asked her. He was sure he would hear on the journey back to *Villefranche*.

It had been so wonderful sitting across from her in the carriage, being alone, talking of whatever they chose. It was not any easier now to suppress his desire for her than a year ago; in fact, it seemed to be getting harder. He knew she understood well the effect of the black willow and she brought it dried and crushed each spring after herb gathering, but it was of little help in suppressing the strong physical feelings. He wondered what she would say if he asked her to give up her vow of chastity. "I will have to make confession for even thinking that!" he thought to himself. His Serene Highness had been displeased with him again at matins. The Bishop was embracing all with "*Surrexit Dominus.*" Paolo had greeted his brothers in the vernacular, "Christ is truly risen," and they had replied, "Thanks be to God." The phrase had always had more meaning for him in his own tongue, but the Bishop had muttered under his breath, "Franciscans!"

Paolo thought of the beauty of the hundreds of candles blazing in the cathedral as he had prayed throughout the night. The two days of fasting and the prayers had given him an extraordinary clarity and trust. His thoughts drifted to St. Bruno and the Carthusians with their solitude and their delight in nature and meditations. Perhaps he should have remained in the monastery, he thought, or not entered the priesthood at all. He remembered his time in Paris at the university before he took the vows. The markets, the quarters where cooked chicken and eggs, cheese, tarts, *patés* and salted herring might be purchased right on the street. And the bathhouses! He had heard those were being closed due to a disease growing among those patronizing the prostitutes. He had been to that section also with his young friends. He had not been a virgin when he entered the order. He remembered one particularly lovely "lady" who took him to her house and bathed with him, lathering him with a soap scented with herbs and later rubbing his entire body with oil . . . . His reverie was interrupted by the beginning of the "Te Deum" and he scolded himself silently.

As his gaze fell on the Bishop, several questions plagued him. What was his connection with Sister Jacqueline? He had not seen her in Lyon and had not asked. Why had he insisted that Janine come to Lyon? It was unusual. Why did he want him to go to Toulouse? Did he want it badly enough to hold Janine as bait? He thought of the many intrigues in the Church over the years. The schism over 150 years ago had weakened the entire fabric of the Church. It was claimed that Urban the Sixth refused to have his authority diminished so the cardinals chose a new Pope. But the Anglos continued to support Urban. When the council decided in 1409 to dispose of both and elect another, there were three Holy Fathers! Each designated as a successor of St. Peter! This was finally resolved in 1414 when the Council at Constance agreed to depose all three, elected Martin the Fifth and he returned to the Holy City. Avignon's glory ended. The palace with its towers of extreme height would no longer have its former prestige. Some of these happenings, he surmised, had started the questionings by the people. The institution that they depended upon and looked to for guidance had shown its weaknesses.

Martin Luther had only ridden the crest of a wave already in motion. The restorations, the libraries, the chapels in Rome did not restore the faith of all the people. Many were ready to listen when the Augustinian monk challenged the indulgences being sold everywhere, and questioned the need for confession, priests and priestly celibacy. "Well, my thoughts are back to celibacy again," thought Paolo. "Perhaps it is better for me to be at the altar instead of in the choir; my thoughts wander." He had decided to instruct the coachers to travel back by way of Clermont-Ferrand where the journey would be slower and, hopefully, safer.

Chapter 15

Summer

S omehow, she knew he would come. She could see him walking slowly along the path through the chestnut and oak trees. As he came nearer, she asked, "How did you find me?"

"I followed my heart," he replied smiling. "Why have you come so far? Do you not fear the evil that awaits in the forests?" he said with mock terror on his face.

Janine smiled. "How can I fear something I've never seen? The trees give me comfort. Is this not a most beautiful place?"

"Truly. *Jardin de* éden. I am Adam and you are Eve," replied Paolo.

Janine just smiled as he made himself comfortable on the grass beside her.

"Sister Janine," he started, and she interrupted.

"We are alone, Paolo; you may call me just 'Janine,'" she said.

"Yes," he replied, "we are."

"*Madame Roquefort's* little *génisse* is growing more beautiful every day," said Janine.

"And plumper, also," he replied.

"What shall we do with two cows when she is grown?" Janine asked.

"The *fille* can be given to someone who has need of a cow," he replied.

"With the peace we've had this summer it is hard to imagine the dissension in other areas. The Calvinist group in Montauban seems to be keeping itself to the south. I've heard there are problems in Toulouse. But I don't want to talk of Protestants and wars. I have talked with each family in the village about the school and all are very excited. With the events of just the past year, they can see the necessity of instruction for their children."

"I would like to teach them St. Bede's prayer," said Janine.

"Do you know it all, by memory?" Paolo asked.

"Of course," she replied, quoting, "'Let me not, O Lord, be puffed up with worldly wisdom, which passes away, but grant me that love which never ceases, that I may not choose to know anything among men but Jesus, and Him crucified. I pray thee, that he upon whom Thou hast graciously given the sweet savor of the words of Thy knowledge, may also possess Thee, Font of all wisdom, and shine forever before thy countenance, Amen.'" Janine paused. "What is your favorite quote, Paolo?"

"Oh, I have many favorites," he replied, "especially in Jesus' teachings, but a part of Numbers 7 comes to mind,

'The Lord bless thee and keep thee.
The Lord make His face to shine upon thee
And be gracious unto thee
The Lord lift up his countenance upon thee
And give thee peace'" quoted Paolo.

They both sat in silence, thinking of the beauty of the quote. "Are you familiar with the fourth chapter of Saint Matthew?" asked Paolo.

"Yes, the temptation of the Christ," replied Janine.

"Why was He tempted?" he asked. "Satan should know the Son of God would not be tempted."

"Well, it does say He was hungry; he did have a body as ours. It also says that the angels came and ministered unto Him. Oh, Paolo, your questions!" she chided gently, smiling.

They sat in silence again. When she glanced up at him, he was staring at her. "You are so very beautiful," he said.

Janine smiled, meeting his eyes with love. The silence between them was ablaze with feeling.

"Our love grows, Janine," Paolo said softly.

"Yes, I know," she replied.

"The Bishop has not requested that you be transferred," he said.

"I don't think he will," replied Janine. "The abbess seemed very pleased to hear of our work with the people here: the delivering of babies, the way I have shown the women how to gather and use the herbs and roots and our self-sufficiency. I feel her opinions carry much weight with the Bishop."

"Not as much weight as the Bishop carries!" he said laughing. Janine laughed too, remembering the bulk and appetite of His Serene Highness. "For a thousand years we have followed St. Augustine's teaching that belief is more important than knowledge - *Credo ut intélligam*," quoted Paolo, "which meant that understanding comes only through belief."

"Where was St. Augustine from? I have forgotten," asked Janine.

"He lived in Carthage in the Roman province in Africa. He was called Bishop of Hippo. That was a most prosperous area, growing much corn in that wonderful climate, having irrigation. It was a peaceful community until Rome fell to Alaric the Goth and Carthage fell to the Vandals coming across from Andalusia. St. Augustine's book, called *The City of God*, was the doctrine taken north in establishing the faith in Gaul.

"Isn't it interesting that one, Martin Luther, entered the Order of Augustinian Hermits. He felt the growing restlessness and realized many like him wanted to understand the truth, not just accept the Pope as the ultimate authority. He believed in the forgiving nature of God. He felt that buying a piece of paper could not bring the remission of guilt as many believed. He was teaching the Psalms at the University of Wittenburg when he became convinced of those premises. Janine, am I like the Protestants because I want to understand? I also believe in the forgiveness of God and the truth of the scriptures."

"Oh, Paolo, how you torture yourself!" Janine replied taking his hand softly in hers.

"Janine, I have read everything Avicenna ever wrote and also the philosopher, Pierre Abelard, neither on the approved list," he said in a whisper.

"And what did Messier Abelard write?" she asked.

"*Sic and Non.*" he replied. "He took 168 statements from the Bible and showed all the arguments for and against the accepted interpretations. It brought out the many inconsistencies between accepted authorities. He said, 'By doubting we come to enquiry, by enquiring we perceive the truth.' The Church did not approve." Paolo lowered his head into his hands and shook it slowly. Then he went on, "I may not agree with all they say, but I understand their arguments and I'm afraid because of this I will not be a good priest."

"If you joined the Protestants, God forbid, could you help the people in this village?" Janine asked.

Paolo looked up quickly. "No, I couldn't. They would probably reject me, if not worse," he replied.

"The people love you. You have restored their faith. You have a mission here to do. Their faith would be destroyed if you changed sides or left the priesthood," she said.

"Well, I'm not really contemplating 'changing sides,' Janine. I'm only saying that I do understand why these ideas have arisen."

"It is good to understand," she concurred. "It is also good to work in the vineyard in which you can do the most good for others, for that is your nature. If you had wanted to please your whims, you would have returned to Toulouse and never taken vows," she countered.

"And I would have never known you and that would be the greatest tragedy of all for me," he said softly. "Is this our destiny? Revelations says, 'If one is destined for captivity, into captivity he goes! If one is destined to be slain by the sword, by the sword he will be slain. Such is the faithful endurance that distinguishes God's holy people.'"

"Somehow that quote makes me feel sad and discomfited. Will you say the Canticle of St. Francis with me before we walk back?" Janine asked.

"Of course," he replied. Together they chanted:
'Most high, omnipotent, good Lord,
To you alone belong praise and glory,
Honor and blessing.
No man is worthy to breathe your name.
Be praised, my Lord, for all your creation.
In the first place for the blessed Brother Sun
Who gives us the day and enlightens us through you.
He is beautiful and radiant with great splendor,
Giving witness of you, most Omnipotent One.
Be praised my Lord, for Sister Moon and the stars
Formed by you so bright, precious and beautiful.
Be praised, my Lord, for Brother Wind
And the airy skies, so cloudy and serene;
For every weather, be praised, for it is life-giving.
Be praised, my Lord, for our sister, Mother Earth,
Who nourishes and watches us
While bringing forth abundant fruits
with colored flowers and herbs.
Praise and bless the Lord.
Render him thanks.
Serve Him with great humility.
Amen.'

"It's even more beautiful when we say it together," Janine said softly.

"How do you always know what to say to make me feel more at peace?" he asked. "Could we stay here forever?"

She just smiled and began gathering up her little cloth bags of leaves, roots and bark pieces. "Mother Marguerite will have to climb all those steps and ring the vespers bell, if you are not there," she said.

103

Chapter 16

Fall

Matins was beautiful this morning, Janine reflected, as she began her daily duties. The dawn was just breaking as prayers ended. They would soon be going to the winter schedule. The early morn was cool now. She reminded herself to be sure to tell Paolo about the *colchis*, the little cowbell-shaped flowers, she had seen on her walk yesterday. The autumn crocus always heralded the coming of winter. She had talked with some of the children herding pigs in the forest who were feasting on the recently fallen chestnuts, acorns and beechnuts. The winter would bring butchering and Paolo always helped those who needed another strong arm.

The children seemed a little apprehensive but eager for the school to begin. It would be only a few weeks now. In the midst of carrying water from the well, Janine paused and gazed at the mountains to the east with the sun just about to rise over them. "So beautiful," she thought, "They soon will have snow on them. The mountains always make me feel stronger. I wonder if St. Francis felt this way about Mt. Subasio." She thought about her unsuccessful search for the nettle plant yesterday. Her grandmother had taught her that it was helpful if visions became upsetting. She had been having, perhaps not visions, but frightening dreams that awakened her in a panic. The scenes were vague, but her pounding heart was very real. The talk going around the village about the group of Jesuits that had been murdered on the coast by the Huguenots may have been the cause of her dreams, she surmised. The new Jesuit order had been recognized at the Assembly of Poissy only two years ago and had already evoked a particular dislike among the Protestants. Now, Father Paolo had said, the English were rallying to aid the Calvinists in the north. He had hinted that he might send the sisters to a convent, perhaps in Cordoba, if the Protestant sieges came any nearer. There were still the rumors of a group nearby to the south. The Kingdom of Castile had not yet been affected by this heresy. But there was yet some unrest between the Church and the Jews in that land. In *Léon*, one execution by fire had been called an 'Act of Faith.' Soon the passes over the mountains would be difficult and she doubted if Sister Clare could withstand such a journey. Clare had spoken less of her affliction since Sister Mary had come to learn from her, but Janine had observed that her bones were more noticeable when she helped her into her daily herbal soak.

Janine began preparing the cracked wheat, thinking of the pilgrimage to Rome that Paolo had spoken of last week. The Bishop apparently had encouraged it, perhaps next summer. He had said the journey should include all, depending on Sister Clare's health, of course. Rome seemed so far away, yet she wanted to see it more than almost any place she could think of, except perhaps St. Leonard. Thoughts of expanses of heather and rolling hills of bracken took her back to the north, the bilberries, and the orphanage in the hills. She wondered about some of the children who were now two years older than when she left. She thought of *Bourgeneuf*, the town to the east that had a large castle with a tower. Rumor was that a Mohammedan prince from Castile was once imprisoned there. And, there was Aubusson; its tapestries were becoming sought after in many countries.

She glanced out the open window to the village below. Smoke was rising from several chimneys. The men had been having meetings, encouraged by Father Paolo. There was talk of making it a village order to always have a bucket of water by every doorway, in case of fire. Two families had laid wide brick walks in front of their home and business. Jon Dyere, a blacksmith, and his wife, Bonne, had bought the vacant stone house at the far edge of the village and were putting an ocher-colored wash on it. Their children, two boys, would be in the school, he had assured them. The Benét brothers had prospered on the land Paolo had helped them clear. The grains were being ground at the mill, and Pons, the miller, had to seek outside markets for all the flour they had. Now, Arnaud Benét was to marry Pons daughter, Vivene. That would be a joyful occasion. Paolo had talked with Vivene many hours, she knew, in and out of the confessional. She was one who had been initiated into the plea-sures of the flesh by Father Tomás and had a difficult time believing anyone would want her for a wife. Janine had talked with her also on two occasions at Paolo's suggestion. She told Vivene of Christ's love for even the harlot. She also spoke of human love and com-mitment. Arnaud was able to see her desire to change; she refused invitations she had once readily accepted. Arnaud was busy these days, with the help of his family and Paolo, building a house on the reclaimed land by the river. Now that the dam was in place, it was a safer place than before.

The Bishop had sent word to them that he was trying to get a clock for their bell tower, but Father Paolo was only tight-jawed about that news. He loved tolling the bell at each office and prob-ably would as long as he could. Janine smiled to herself, thinking about him. She thought of St. John's quote of Christ as she set bowls on the table in the refectory, "Peace I leave with you, my peace, I give unto you . . ."

A sudden clatter of horses hooves on the cloister stones broke her reverie and she was about to go to the side door when a great crash in the chapel made her realize that someone on horseback had burst into the nave. She heard Mother Marguerite scream. A man with a torch burst through the side door. Janine ran out through the back door wondering where Sister Mary was. It was obvious these men meant to harm. If she could run to the forest maybe she would be safe, she thought.

Father Paolo heard the commotion below and glanced up from his reading. There appeared to be a lot more smoke in the valley and village than usual. Then he heard a crash and a scream from the chapel. He jumped up and as he ran for the door, out of the north window, he caught a glimpse of Janine running across the meadow; a horseman was pursuing her. "Oh, dear God!" he invoked and crashed down the stairs. At the bottom, he smelled the smoke, but dashed out the back door. He could not see Janine; the stables were in the way. He grabbed a walking staff and ran as fast as he could.

Janine glanced back; smoke was coming from the roof of the church. A man on horseback was nearing her. She ran as fast as she could, the skirt of her habit almost tripping her. She heard hoof beats near. The man leapt from the horse, knocking her down. It took the air out of her; she was dazed. When her vision cleared, the man was rolling her over and saying something she could not understand, but she understood the look in his eyes. He ripped her habit open at the torso and tore off her headpiece. Her long hair tumbled out. He tugged at her undergarments and grabbed her breast, grunting approval. She struggled fiercely and tried to turn and pull away. He cursed and hit her savagely on the side of her head with the back his closed fist. She lay dazed, scarcely aware that he was clumsily trying to find her body under all the many folds and layers in her habit. His larger body on top of her was nearly crushing her. It seemed hard to breathe; she struggled futilely. Her head hurt so badly. He had managed to find her legs and part them and was ripping at her undergarments when he became aware of a sound behind him. He turned to see Father Paolo coming at him with raised staff. The man whirled on his knees, and grabbing his sword, impaled the priest, as Janine screamed "No!!"

Paolo fell to the side as the man jerked his sword out and turned back to the nun. She fought now with every ounce of strength she had left in her. A sound from the church caught his attention; he turned. His companions were shouting at him.

Janine thought she could see some of the village men coming up the hill. "Aach!" he grunted as he rose, grabbing his horse's reins nearby. He picked up his sword and glanced at her briefly; shaking his head, he slashed the sword across the side of her neck. Jumping on his horse, he pushed it into a gallop without looking back.

Janine grabbed her neck; it felt very warm. Then the realization came with each pulsation. It began to grow dark. "But it is morning," she thought. A sound to her right caught her attention. Paolo painfully and slowly inched nearer with great effort. She reached out to him and clasped his hand. Peace began to flow over her. There was no pain. Their hands lay together on the crushed *colchis* flowers that had harkened the beginning of winter.

Part Two

Chapter 1

Fall

The late sun cast golden tints across her face as she leaned back against the side of the hot tub, eyes closed. The upper half of her perfect breasts was visible above the water.

"Jan, you are so beautiful," said Paul. "You look like an Egyptian queen with your hair pulled up that way."

Jan opened her eyes halfway and smiled at him, "Why couldn't I have met you twenty years ago?"

"We weren't ready for each other then," he replied.

"I can't tell you how wonderful it feels to be with you," said Jan.

"It seems that if I could understand how we were drawn to each other I would understand the entire universe," said Paul.

"Yes, the mysteries of the universe . . ." she said with eyes closed. "I've spent the larger part of my adult life searching and I feel no closer to discovery."

"You may have discovered more than you realize," he replied smiling. "I submit as evidence this beautiful happy day."

"But look where I was only three years ago - lost, lonely, feeling like giving up. I'm sure you remember that morning," she said.

"I'll never forget it! I still don't know why I woke up early and decided to go on into the office or why I took the long route that morning. But when I saw you standing on the overlook by the canyon, some automatic control took over."

"I can't even remember driving there," she offered, "I remember waking at around 4:00 or 5:00 with another migraine. It was so bad that I wasn't sure I could make it to the medicine cabinet. I doubted I could keep down medication; I was already so nauseated. I seemed to have no real thoughts, just feelings, physical pain and emotional pain - just some blind intent that I would not live the rest of my life that way. I don't even remember getting in the car or driving; I just knew I did not want to go to the ER again. It was as though I also was on auto pilot, like you just said. I remember noticing what a beautiful summer morning it was as I looked into that canyon. Then thoughts of Lynn at college, those were the thoughts that were holding me there. I think her entire childhood ran through my mind. Then somewhere in my fog a man was saying, "Beautiful morning, isn't it?" She looked at him smiling.

"Well, what do you say to a lady, poised on the edge of a canyon, crying?"

"I remember what you said. You said very softly, 'You're much too beautiful to cry.'"

"Well, I wondered if I had stepped into a movie set. I even looked around for a cameraman. You looked like a model posed there.

"But when your eyes met mine," she said seriously, looking into his deep blue eyes, "there seemed to be no words for either of us. All the questions disappeared and all the answers took their place as though they had always been there. When you asked if I would like to get some breakfast, it was as if we stepped out of some eternal reality back into this dimension. I felt almost dizzy like my head was empty and I had come out of some time warp."

"Well, when I said to myself, 'Hell, I'll just go on in to work, can't sleep,' I didn't expect my whole life to change," he said laughing. "We've come a long way in three years."

"Yes, my migraines are slightly better. Oh, I've been intending to tell you about a new therapy I read about called past life regression. I may try it," Jan said.

"Well, the work you've done with relaxation and visualization has helped a lot," Paul offered.

"I know what has helped me - your love has been a miracle," she said softly as she made her way lazily across the hot tub and knelt between his legs.

"Why have they not gone away then? I think I must give you more love!" he said pulling her closer. "I think first, though, we must get out of this water before we both look like prunes!" He took her hands and pulled her to her feet. The sun had dropped behind the purple mountains. She shivered as she grabbed for the towels.

"We'll dry off in the bedroom," he said as he scooped her and the towels up in his arms and carried them inside.

The fiery colors of the turning leaves lost their heat in the fading light.

Chapter 2

Winter

"Who? At Mercy Hospital?" Janine asked as she answered the phone.

"What?!" she gasped.

"An accident? Oh my God! I'll be there in fifteen minutes! Yes, thank you." Jan replaced the receiver with trembling hands and dashed to the closet for her coat and bag. She almost tripped running down the steps to the garage. The car didn't care that she was frantic. It took its usual 'good ol' easy time' as she strained at the key. A light snow was falling but was melting as it touched the pavement, still warm in the fading light.

"Oh, dear God, please don't let anything happen to him," she prayed. "Please let us be together at least a while. I have just found him again."

Horns blared as she passed in a tight spot. She scarcely noticed. Her thoughts were on Paul; her driving was on automatic. Was he hurt badly? "I should have asked more questions," she chided herself. "Oh, shoulda, woulda, coulda! Only a few minutes now," she thought.

She screeched to a stop in the parking lot nearest the emergency room and ran into the bright light. "I'm Jan Miller," she said breathlessly to the nurse at the desk, "Someone called, my husband . . ."

"Oh, yes, Mrs. Miller, please come this way," said the nurse with a totally calm face as she led her into a room inside the ER doors.

Tears came to her eyes when she saw him on the table covered with a sheet. She rushed to his side. "Oh, darling, are you hurt badly?"

"Jan, you shouldn't have rushed so; I'm o.k." said Paul smiling. "The x-rays show a couple of broken ribs, and a few bruises."

"Your forehead is cut," she observed. "What happened?"

"I think the man may have had a bit too much liquor and just didn't see the stop sign. Sweetie, I am fine. We will go as soon as they finish the paperwork and I can get my clothes back," he said, wincing as he tried to sit up nonchalantly.

"Well, so much for being graceful for a few days," he laughed. "Oohh, and so much for laughing too!" he said in a more serious tone.

Later, when she had very carefully helped him into the passenger seat of the car, she asked, "Your car? Was it totaled?"

"No, I had it towed to Murphey's; I think it can be repaired," he replied. "It's just the doors and the side. I'll talk with them tomorrow."

"From your bedside phone," she said firmly as she started up the car. "Oh, darling, I was so scared. To lose you after having you only three years would be more than I could take." Tears began to run down Janine's cheeks.

"There, there," he said, trying to put his arm around her and finding it more painful than he expected. "You're not going to lose me. It was a simple accident. I will have a good excuse to hang out at the house for a few days. Perhaps we can go somewhere. It will be good for both of us to go some place warm for a while. What do you say? Can you get away? Any deadlines?" he asked.

"No, not really. It sounds wonderful," she said sniffling and dabbing at her eyes. "What about the blueprints you are working on? Can they wait?"

"If they want me for the architect, it can!" he replied.

"Where shall we go?" she asked.

"Will you let me surprise you?" he asked.

"Well, you'll have to tell me what to pack," Jan replied.

"Ummmm, pack casual clothes . . . for a warm climate; oh yes, bring that 'skimpy' swim suit!"

"Oh you! I love you so much!" she said trying to hug him with her right arm without hurting him anywhere.

After a couple of minutes, he asked, "Jan, do you believe there are no accidents? That we draw to us all the things that happen? That somehow, for some reason, I, myself, put me in that intersection for a reason? Is it karma? Or low vibes? Mind somewhere else?"

"Well, yes, I guess I believe that. I don't understand it, but it makes sense to me. If we are slightly out of alignment with the universe, in which case our vibratory rate would be lower because we would not be channeling as much universal energy, and if we are not in sync, the universe, working with our inner selves, encourages us to pay attention and come back into the full experience of the perfection of the universe."

"Uh huh," he stared at her, nodding his head, trying to grasp what his non-alignment might be.

"Anyway, that's how I understand it. I'm sure it's a lot more complicated than that," Jan went on.

"No, I think I have been going along, rather unaware, unthankful, for several months. How nice of the universe to send me a little 'message'. Let's go home." He smiled as she kissed him quickly on the nose.

"I'm so glad you chose this hotel," said Jan. "I could just sit here and watch the waves forever."

"It's great the way this lounge overlooks the ocean. I've heard whales can be seen from here this time of year. I wish we had brought the binoculars up with us," replied Paul.

"Wouldn't that be wonderful?! I still can't believe you chose this place. I never mentioned to you that I was doing some research on cetaceans and the Sea of Cortez, did I? My agent suggested a possible article or book with photographs, but I had sort of put it in the back of my mind. I hope I can get some good photos. Do you think we could hire one of the fishing boats to take us out to look for dolphins? Or would that rocking about be too much on the ribs?" she asked.

"No, no, I'm feeling fine. We'll walk down to the dock tomorrow morning and see what we can find out. Another pina colada?" he asked her as the waiter approached.

"No," she replied, "one's my limit before dinner. Speaking of which . . ."

"Yes, me too." "Can we order dinner out here?" he asked the waiter.

"*Si,*" replied the young man.

"Great! Could we see a menu?" Paul asked.

"So," he went on when the waiter left, "tell me about the Sea of Cortez, or Mar del Sur, or South Sea, as it used to be called."

"Aha!" exclaimed Jan, "I see you've been doing some research too. Sometimes I'm amazed at how our minds run along the same track."

"Well, it has also been called the Vermillion Sea, because of the plankton growth at times, she continued. "This Baja was called the Isthmus of Tehuantepec. Don't ask me why! I didn't find that out. After conquering all of New Spain, Hernando Cortés wanted to explore the Pacific coast so he started building ships around 1525. I'm not sure why it took ten years, but we think in terms of how fast things get done today. Anyway, in 1535, he led an expedition from the mainland across the Sea to what is now La Paz - the city of peace. There were other explorers after that; most had heard of the pearls the natives wore and petitioned the viceroy for exclusive rights to pearl hunting there. Many were not prepared for the expense and difficulties involved so the efforts failed, for the most part. But a familiarity with this Sea came out of the efforts and they learned that this was not an island and that they had to come all the way around this very cape we are looking upon to go up to the Californias."

"When did the missionaries come here?" asked Paul.

"I think most all expeditions had a priest or two, but in the 1660s, Captain Francisco de Lucenilla applied to His Excellency, the viceroy, for rights to exploration and pearl hunting, but he had to agree to take two priests along. There was quite a clamor between the Jesuits and the Franciscans as to who should have the right to 'missionize' this new territory. The bishopric of Guadelajara considered the Californias part of its diocese. Anyway, it was decided in favor of the Franciscans and both priests selected had recently come over from Spain. I guess there was considerable conflict between the priests' mission and that of the captain and the pearl hunters. The journey from what we know as Mazatlan today to here, took six days and they reported seeing whales on that journey. That must have been exciting! The natives had only reed canoes called balsas and the pearls they traded for knives were poorly shaped and grayish in color. The natural pearls are usually not like what we see in the jewelry stores, the cultured pearls. Oh, here is dinner already."

"I read Peter Benchley's book about the girl of the Sea of Cortez; found it fascinating. Have you read it?" asked Paul.

"No, I'll have to try to find it when we get home. Do you have a copy? I don't remember seeing it in our library," Jan asked.

"No, I think a girlfriend loaned it to me," he replied.

"A girl friend, huh?" she said teasing him.

"The trip down was pleasant wasn't it?" Paul said, ignoring her taunt.

"That was slick!" she laughed.

"Do you want to talk of ex spouses, girlfriends and lovers?" he asked in a 'hum drum' tone.

"No! I'm just teasing you," she said laughing. "I think we covered all that quite thoroughly the first few times we went out. It seemed like we talked about everything, like old friends, catching up on years apart. And, yes, it was a lovely trip. I just felt a little intimidated by all the soldiers and officials at the airport. I really didn't preconceive anything, but I guess I just expected it to be like in the States, not walk across the edge of the landing field, seeing automatic weapons. But I've always wanted to come down here. Do you want to fish if we can get a boat?" Jan asked.

"No, I'm really not into that kind of fishing. I understand the striped marlin come in the spring and there might be a few around. No, I enjoy a game of hide and seek with a trout and a fly line, but to take an animal nearly twice as big as myself - what would I do with it? I can't eat it! It would seem barbaric to hang it on the wall in the house, assuming I could even catch something and land it with these ribs!" he said laughing. "No, I prefer to leave them in the Sea. By the way, did you know the Baja was formed when the San Andreas Fault split it off from the mainland?"

"When was that?" Jan asked mock-innocently.

"Oh, a few days ago - or was it a few million years?" Paul said laughing.

He suddenly leaned closer to her across the table and said in a low voice, "Jan, I'm sorry I've not been able to be much of a lover since the accident."

"Why, darling, there's no need to apologize. You know our love is much more than just physical. I can't tell you how much I've enjoyed these days we've been able to be together every day. You know, this is the first time since our honeymoon that we've spent this much uninterrupted time together."

"This isn't exactly like our honeymoon, is it?" he said laughing softly.

"What a wonderful, sexy time we had!" she replied. "Was the Maine coast ever so filled with love? I think we could have lit all the lighthouses – by just hooking a line to our toes! You sexy man, I love you. Do you know what my greatest dream is?"

"To go back to Penobscot Bay?" he said laughing.

"No, to be able to spend every day with you," said Jan, looking into his eyes with love.

"Well, we'll be able to retire in ten to fifteen years, if all goes well," he replied.

"I want it *now*, while we are still young, well, sort of young. I guess one couldn't call a man who is going to be a grandfather in two months 'young,' but we are pretty lively!"

"I still can hardly believe that Jon and Sandi are expecting a baby. But I say you're as young as you feel."

"Well, for an 'old man' you surely are the most exciting man I've ever known," said Jan.

"So, how are we to make your dream come true?" he asked.

"Well, you know about visualization?" she replied.

"Sure, it's what I do when you have clothes on and I close my eyes and. . ."

"Shushh, you're making me crazy," she said giggling. "Everything in the world was created by thought, alright? Everything is energy. 'Energy goes from unmanifest to materialized by thought.' I am quoting from a book I read by someone named Patent. O.K., so thoughts create. We are going to create our lives for the next twenty-five years, so, why not create them just as we want them? So, if we change our thoughts, beliefs, and feelings and visualize exactly what we want, we can have it. That is the teaching anyway."

"It sounds too simple and easy," Paul said.

"Well, it involves listening to our intuition, like we did, perhaps, on the day we met. And, it seems, we have to align with universal principles such as love, peace and the perfection of the universe. No, I don't think it is easy. Trusting in the perfection of the universe is not easy. At times, the world seems like such a cruel and bizarre place. To feel oneness with everything seems impossible," said Jan.

"We are not asked to feel oneness with prisons, the judicial system or the latest rock group, are we?" he asked laughing. "Just the creation, which includes all persons, right?" he asked. "The things I mentioned are created by humans out of the ego."

"Yes, as I said, it's not simple, but the idea has really been occupying my brain lately," she replied.

"I'm not sure I'm ready to 'retire,'" he said, gesturing quotation marks in the air with his fingers. "I love my work and feel it's what I have to contribute to the world."

"I feel the same way about writing and photography, but I also want more time with you. What can we do? Give up sleeping?" she asked.

"Not tonight, please," he said yawning politely. "I feel rather beat."

"I agree; and I'm noticing that the evenings are quite cool here. I should have brought a sweater from the room. Let's sign the check and find our warm bed. Maybe we will think of 'kinky' things to do to a person with broken ribs," said Jan with a mischievous smile and lifted eyebrows.

⌒◌

"Do you think we will see any dolphins, Capitan?" asked Jan.

"Si," he replied. "I usually see them this time of year."

"Can you believe the color of this water?" she said, looking at Paul. "It's like a blue topaz, and the sky is almost as brilliant. Are we in the Sea or the Pacific, Capitan?" she asked.

"We are in the Sea, del mar, *señora*," the skipper replied.

"I'm so pleased that you can speak English; I'm afraid our *espanól* is quite 'rusty'." said Jan. "I notice many people here speak English."

"Si," he smiled. "It is most necessary; many *turistas* and few speak our language."

Jan went aft and sat by Paul. "Are you doing alright, darling?" she asked.

"Oh, yes. Enjoying everything immensely," he replied. "Although, I must admit I've always been slightly uneasy on large expanses of water."

"You swim well; where do you suppose that uneasiness comes from?" she pondered.

"Have no idea. I've never had a bad experience. Though I don't think I could swim well today," Paul said with a frown.

She smiled at him and their eyes met in their usual telepathic way. "I'm so glad we could arrange this boat, and quite reasonably too. It was too bad that couple that we met at the hotel, what was their name, Hutchins? - couldn't come along. How awful that they both came down with Montezuma's Revenge."

"Yes, they seemed like a lot of fun. Where were they from? Des Moines? It felt good to 'bump into' someone not interested in sport fishing. That's all one hears in the bar!" said Paul.

"I'm so excited to see dolphins! Did you know . . . now, stop rolling your eyes up, you're teasing me. I know you want to know this!" Jan broke down in laughter as Paul burst out laughing, holding onto his ribs.

"Seriously, now, dolphins have in some cultures been almost deified. They were given special reverence because they were supposed to be the ones who assisted persons on the journey into life after death. Isn't that a great picture in the mind?"

"Yes, when was that?" asked Paul.

"Well, Aristotle commented on them in the 4th century BC, but there was a small, fairly unknown culture that developed a little later than this, maybe around 200 or 300 BC, called the Nabateans, that built quite an impressive little empire. They had been nomadic, possibly in Arabia, but they settled in an area of northern Arabia -- east of Egypt and near Syria. The excavations done south of the Dead Sea have turned up some pretty surprising architecture. Many of their statues and sculptures of deities have dolphins and/or fish somewhere on them. The dolphin is seen over and over, yet their civilization was mostly inland and had no ports on the Mediterranean, though it wasn't far away. This little culture was overrun and absorbed into the great Roman Empire, but the idea of the significance of dolphins giving safety and succor on any voyage, especially at sea, continued for centuries, all the way from Iran to England. One sees it popping up in religious symbols all through history." Jan paused.

"That's fascinating; and I apologize for teasing you," Paul said smiling.

"I love it when you tease me," she said. "So, I will bore you some more. There are frescoes on the Queen's Palace excavated at Knossos on the island of Crete that have dolphin pictures that have been identified as the Blue-white Striped Dolphin. This palace is thought to date to 2000 BC. This same species of dolphin; has been spotted as far south as here in the Pacific, but it is rare in the northeastern Atlantic. We probably won't see that one. These, along with the spinner and the spotted dolphins are the ones that are becoming so endangered by the tuna industry."

"Why would the tuna boats harm them?" he asked

"Well, they don't, intentionally. It's just that the large schools of yellow fin tuna often swim directly beneath the dolphin herds."

"They call them 'herds'?" he interrupted incredulously.

"Yes," she said laughing. "That is how they spot them. The larger boats have a plane that accompanies them to help spot fish when they are working nearer the coasts. Anyway, they put out what is called a purse seine - it is huge - sometimes almost a mile long. When they draw it in, many dolphins are trapped and die or are crushed in the power blocks that draw up the net," her voice faltered. "They need to breathe once or twice a minute and the longest they can hold is seven minutes."

"Darling, you have tears in your eyes!" said Paul. "I had no idea you were so fond of these animals."

"They seem more than mere animals, Paul," Jan said sadly, "from all I've read. Their intelligence is just now being studied and communication with them is being attempted. Of course, it's easy to let oneself get carried away, but they do have a larger brain in proportion than human species."

"Just the dolphins?" he asked.

"No, all cetaceans: whales, porpoises too. One man from Greenpeace went aboard one of these ships as a worker. He could hear the dolphins, maybe 500 at a time, shrieking in panic as they were caught in the net; said it was something he would never forget. Of course, that organization is working to get this stopped on an international level. But the large food corporations have a lot of power. The Marine Mammal Protection Act of 1972 has gradually brought the quota of 'accidental' kills down to 20,000 per year, but how can all this be inspected or enforced? And there are few regulations in other countries; so, the tuna boats are just re-flagging to other countries like some in South America. So, it is going to take quite a worldwide effort. Well, now you know why we haven't had much tuna lately. I read that the Albacore are not usually caught in this way, so that's all I buy."

"Well, I'll go along with that. But why don't the dolphins just get out of there when the boats start putting out nets? I've heard they can swim up to 30 miles per hour."

"Dolphins are very timid and easily frightened. The power-boats that put out the nets tend to herd all together in the circular motion of putting out the net. The dolphins exhibit distinct behavior changes under stress. In shallow areas, some have been known to bury their head in the sand when frightened by the noise of the boats. Even if they are released alive from the nets, the stress may be enough to kill them. These large ships can bring in enough tuna in one voyage to be worth a million dollars. So, the U.S. is still responsible for more dolphin deaths than any other country even with its laws. It is estimated that 3 to 5 million were killed in a fifteen-year period in the last century."

"That's pretty sick for our 'advanced culture' isn't it?" said Paul.

"As far as I can find, a dolphin has never hurt a single human. No matter what we do, they never retaliate. And they could! Many weigh over 200 pounds and have about 150 teeth. And, this has been another reason they were killed - for their teeth! In the Solomon Islands, the people would make necklaces out of 1000 dolphin teeth; this took six or seven animals. The meat was usually wasted and the necklace sold for $50. That's placing a $6.00 value on each dolphin. Paul, dolphin pairs have been seen swimming with their pectoral fins overlapping like holding hands."

"There they are!" shouted the Captain, pointing over starboard. They both stood up.

"Oh, yes. Oh, they are so graceful and sleek," said Jan.

"We will go nearer," said the captain. Soon, two pairs were cruising in the bow wake.

"They seem so carefree. Are these the Bottlenose, *Capitan Ortega*?" Jan asked as she photographed quickly with the digital camera.

"No, *señora*, they are the common dolphin. See the gray pattern like *ocho* on the side?" he replied.

"Oh yes, see his white tummy?" she said. "How many are on that side, Paul?"

"Oh, I would say near a hundred. They seem to be feeding on something in the water. What do they eat?"

"Anchovies, squid - this may be anchovies," replied the captain. "They eat thousands and thousands."

"Have you seen schools, uh, herds, larger than this, Capitan?" Paul asked.

"Oh yes, much larger. But I have talked to some fishermen who have seen very large groups - they say thousands; and they are known to be reliable. It would go on for miles," he replied.

"Jan, I had a friend who was fishing with his own boat near Guaymas across on the mainland. He said they were traveling out toward an island going about ten to twelve miles an hour and suddenly there was a long line of dolphins on either side of them almost as far as they could see in both directions and perhaps five or six deep. And the dolphins passed them up as though they had someplace to get to!" said Paul.

"Really?! That must have been something to see! Come over here, darling; look at this sweet one, leaping beside the boat. She looked right at me! In the eye, Paul!"

"Why do you say 'she'?" he asked.

"I don't know. She just seemed to be. See her up there in the wake. See, she is a little smaller than the others."

"Maybe it's a juvenile," he offered.

"Well I don't know. I think I read that juveniles are sort of pushed out of the adult pod and form their own pod after they are weaned. They don't become sexually mature till they are six to nine years old. OH! Look at that one! He must have gone 15 feet in the air. They are just showing off for us now, it seems," said Jan.

"They are a joyful animal, *señora*," said Captain Ortega.

"Oh, they are going back with the others now," she said. "Can we stay with them, *Capitan*?"

"Of course, *señora*, I am at your service," said Ortega as he swung the craft around to the right.

When they were nearer, a dozen came over to leap around the boat. Jan was snapping photos furiously.

"I'll never forget this day, Paul," she said staring at their sleek bodies.

"Can you hear their little calls or 'talking'?" asked Paul.

"Barely. Can we shut off the engine for a minute, Capitan?" she asked.

"Of course," he replied touching the switch.

Jan held out her hand to the dolphin playing by the boat. The dolphin stood upright in the water as if sniffing her hand; then opened his mouth, made a noise and dived again. Jan was so awestruck she couldn't speak. "Oh, Oh . . . . Paul," she stammered as she looked around.

"Yes, I saw it, Jan, and got a photo," he said laughing. "I think he wants to know who you are."

"His look was so intelligent. It was not like looking a cat in the eyes at all. There seems to be, a . . . a . . . sharing or understanding. Oh, they are moving away now."

"Shall we follow, *señor*?" asked the captain. Paul looked at Jan with questioning eyebrows.

"No, I feel like we are invading their dining room. But this has been so special!" said Jan. "This makes me think of what Plutarch said, 'The dolphin has a gift longed for by the greatest philosophers - unselfish friendship.'"

"When did Plutarch live? I've forgotten," asked Paul.

"Oh, he was in the first century, some years after the death of Christ. Another thing I read was about the Maori's of New Zealand, who thought that dolphins were the messengers of the gods. There have been incidents all through history of dolphins helping persons in danger in the seas. Pliny wrote of one that befriended a boy floundering at sea and bore him back to land and stayed around the bay, becoming quite famous. Someone secretly put him to death according to Pliny. It seems to always happen that way. Jacques Cousteau wrote of one who made friends with the divers around La Corogna, Spain. They named her Niña and she became a national attraction at the beach. Her corpse was found on the beach one day. Almost every incident of dolphins coming into the bays, staying for extended periods and interrelating with humans, has ended in this way. Sometimes I'm ashamed of my own species."

"Shall we head back, *señor*?" asked the captain.

"Yes, *Capitan Ortega*. We've had our dolphin experience," said Paul, smiling at Jan who was leaned back against the side of the boat, eyes closed in complete reverie.

"Darling, you are glowing," said Paul.

"I know, I feel such happiness here," she replied.

"Yes, but you are also physically glowing. You had best put on your hat or you might burn," he said.

"Oh, yes," she said, grabbing for her boat hat that lay on the seat beside her. "I would have been going to the tanning salon if I'd known we were coming *here*."

"It's nice that the winds are calm today. I've heard they can get some nasty storms here," said Paul. "*Chubascos* - eh, *Capitan*?"

"Si, *señor*," replied Ortega, "A time to stay in one's bed! Oh, *señora*, see the terns? There, starboard. Those are white Elegant Terns, seen only in this sea," he said, pointing.

"Very beautiful, Capitan," said Jan. "Do you ever see manta rays?"

"Si, señora, some are poisonous, but I hardly ever hear of anyone being stung. I have heard there are thirty different kinds of sharks here, but I see only a few."

"I read that in the 50s twenty-two sperm whales beached themselves in the shallows off La Paz," she said.

"*Si, señora*. It was still being talked about when I was a child. They said the stench was almost unbearable. The people worked day and night trying to salvage and process what they could, but, of course, most was left to rot."

"What is the tide difference here, *Capitan*?" asked Paul.

"About *tres* feet, *señor*," replied Ortega, maneuvering his craft as he spoke. "At the north end, the tide can vary as much as 23 feet."

"Very interesting. Jan, do you know what a 'bore' is?" Paul asked.

"Oh, we are going to play twenty questions, eh? A bore is a male pig," she said laughing.

"Wrong! I'm speaking of a 'tidal bore.' The tide from the Pacific goes all the way up the Sea of Cortez in five and half hours, hits the north end where the Colorado River dumps in and for a little while the rush causes the river to flow backward. That is a *bore*."

"I can think of still another kind of a 'bore'!" she said laughing. Paul laughed with her.

"Well, we won't have time to go down to the beach tonight will we? The sun is getting low. But perhaps time for a nice Jacuzzi tub soak before dinner. If I can stay awake. This sea air is really relaxing," said Jan.

Chapter 3

Spring

"I'm so glad you suggested a special dinner at home instead of going out," Jan said as she spread a fresh linen tablecloth and placed silver candleholders on the table. "It seems we've had so little time together since we came back from Mexico. We've both been so busy and tired."

"I still feel badly about not changing our flight to the next day or even the following. I feel so powerless when you have a migraine," said Paul.

"Darling, I know you want to make my life perfect in every way, but this problem is one I must solve. When I feel one coming on, I have just one thought: to get to my bed as soon as possible. I didn't want to spoil the memory of our beautiful vacation by having a headache there," she replied.

"Do you think the thought of leaving that paradise caused enough tension to bring on the headache?" he asked.

"I wish I knew, love. I'm studying and considering everything I can imagine from food allergies to insanity," said Jan.

"Dear," he said, turning her around gently and taking her in his arms, "you are no where near insanity. You are one of the most balanced persons I know."

"Well, I do have a tendency to go from being an absolute workaholic when I'm on a project to complete inertia at times. Some would call that manic-depressive or bi-polar but my psychologist explored the lithium connection with my doctor. My blood tests were perfect. Ummm, this smells wonderful. I love it when you cook," she said.

"I know how you like stir-fry, so I dreamed up this one with chicken and your favorite vegetables – voila' - red peppers, snow peas, scallions, water chestnuts. We'll see how it turns out," Paul said stirring the food.

"So, they liked your article on Cabo San Lucas?" he asked. "I haven't had a chance to read it, but the photographs turned out great, I thought!" he said placing the plates and silver on the table.

"Yes, I was pleased. I included some excerpts about the playful nature of dolphins that have been observed in bays and those remaining near populated areas. The dolphins seem to show a curious lack of inhibition when they get to know people. I mentioned two males in particular, one in Napier, New Zealand and another around San Salvador island in the Bahamas, who would get an erection when playing around the divers. And a female on the coast of Spain would rub her genital area against a diver's extended hand. They seem so free in their expression of themselves. Did I mention to you that there has been some cross breeding between species in captivity?"

"No, do you mean between various kinds of dolphins?" he asked.

"Also, in one instance, between a pilot whale and a Tursiops dolphin," she continued. "This produces a hybrid calf. Apparently, though, this never happens in the wild.

"How long do dolphins usually live?" he asked.

"Well, that was another thing I mentioned in the article. There is quite a range in the estimates -- some say 18 years, others say fifty. It's a new area of exploration."

"I'm so glad you've been able to bring some of these facts to a new audience, especially about the danger these intelligent animals are in. Well, our entrée is ready. The rice is in the steamer; the candles are lit. Oh, yes, one moment. I shall return," he said as we went out the door to the garage.

"Oh, you shouldn't have!" Jan exclaimed as he came in with a huge vase of long stemmed yellow roses and white daisies. "They're gorgeous!"

Paul put them on the table. "They're to let you know how much you brighten up my life." He kissed her softly, "Happy birthday."

"You sweetheart! What can I say?" They ate in silence a minute, and then she said, "My mother called."

"Really? How is she?" he asked.

"Seems to be fine. They've had a lot of rain in Atlanta, but it's beginning to feel like spring," she said. "Ummm, this is delicious, just the right amount of tamari. She had a letter from my father. It seems he is out this way, around Denver somewhere. He wanted to see me and asked for our address," said Jan, a look of concern coming across her face.

"It's been years, hasn't it, Jan, since you've seen him?"

"Yes, I think Lynn was small, the last time. He left us when I was nine. I was always afraid of him, though he never laid a hand on me, not even a spanking. When he was sober, he seemed to be in awe of me, like a fragile piece of china that would break; and when he was drunk, I was kept away from him by my mother. How they ever got together, I will never know. They were so different: she religious - he a rich, carefree drunk. Perhaps the drinking wasn't evident at first, and perhaps she has grown more orthodox over the years," said Jan.

"How do you feel about seeing him again?" he asked.

"I don't know. Scared maybe. I guess I'm wondering what he wants. From what I understand he drank up much of his inheritance long ago," she said. "Anyway, I don't want to even think about that tonight. This is much too special to spoil with worrisome thoughts. Is your project almost finished?"

"The church? Yes, almost. I can't believe the changes we've had on this one. I almost told them to find someone else two weeks ago," said Paul.

"It's interesting to me that you, a 'non-religious' shall we say, has acquired such a reputation in church architecture," Jan said between bites.

"I find it hard to understand, myself. These recent ones have everything from gymnasiums to video rooms. They are becoming cities within themselves, like in the Middle Ages when the monasteries were complete communities. I've studied the layouts and construction of many in Europe and find them fascinating. Would you like to visit some one day? Would you be interested at all in a trip like that?" he asked.

"I'd love it! You know my interest in the history of religions, which, by the way, was a subject my mother didn't bring up this time. I don't know if that is the cause, but there always seems to be an invisible barrier between us; it's hard to explain. It's like our love bumps into 'something' before it gets to the other person."

"She is so opposed to my belief in reincarnation that I never bring it up anymore. I have tried to explain to her that the Nicean Council deleted from their version of the Bible some of the references to many lives, and that Emperor Justinian and Empress Theodosia in the sixth century had any remaining references to reincarnation taken out of the Bible. But she maintains that what we have today is what God wanted us to have. So, what can I say? I could quote, Revelations 3:12, 'Him that overcometh will I make a pillar in the temple of my god and he shall go out no more.' And, in one sense, I agree, in part, with her in a round about way, that it seems Jesus lived to bring a new way of thinking and living. If one could fully live the life of love he taught, they might attain enlightenment or 'samadi,' as they say in the Orient and 'be lifted off the wheel of karma.' But, I'm not sure that means we won't want to come again. Emmet Fox felt that the reason Jesus didn't teach much about life-death cycles was that he didn't want people to procrastinate until the next lifetime to begin elevating their lives or consciousness."

"Well, the scripture does say 'As you sow, so shall you reap,'" said Paul.

"Yes, most people think of karma as punishment. Actually, I think it is just a needed 'upgrade' that we choose to draw into our awareness. We always have free will, a choice; we can learn from the lesson or we can take it again next semester, so to speak. The ways of the universe are never vindictive, just consistent. Universal laws are perfect and more patient than we can ever imagine," Jan said smiling.

"In other words, we return to advance our level of consciousness, raise our vibrational rate, as some would say, or move closer to the perfected state?" he added.

"Yes, we try to teach ourselves to rise above negative habit patterns such as fear or hatred or revenge. We must connect with our 'soul self' and reprogram our subconscious. Some say that prayer is an act in reprogramming."

"I've always thought that child prodigies were proof enough of reincarnation. Take Chopin, for example, one of his concerts was publicly performed when he was nine, Beethoven at age eight, and Shubert was composing at eleven," said Paul.

"I read somewhere that 23% of all Americans believe in rebirth, and 28% in Britain; yet, 67% of Americans believe in life after death. I wonder where they think their eternal soul was before birth. Or, if they've read Jeremiah, the first chapter that quotes God as saying, 'Before I formed thee in the belly, I knew thee.'"

"Or how do they explain the thousands and thousands of people who have remembered previous lifetimes either under hypnosis or just spontaneously?" added Paul.

"They ignore it. It's called blocking out what doesn't jive with your picture of the world. It is refusing to broaden your horizons. I'm sorry, that sounds 'tacky' and judgmental. Each person is where he or she is and to love is to accept that. But enough of that; I want you to know how much I've enjoyed this dinner and the conversation. It was great!" said Jan.

"Oh, it's not over yet, birthday girl. Come and sit by me on the couch; I have another little surprise for you," he said leading her by the hand and giving her a small package as she sat down.

Jan opened it carefully, looking at him sideways from time to time with a question in her eyebrows. "Oh, Paul!" she whispered as she opened the case. "You shouldn't have. It's real." The emerald in the ring setting sparkled.

"Yes, it is. I heard you say once how much you liked emeralds."

"It's so beautiful; I'm afraid to touch it."

"Here," he said, taking the ring from the case and placing it on her right hand, "let's see if it fits."

"It's perfect. You had the size from our wedding bands, didn't you? It looks so expensive, love; you shouldn't have," said Jan.

"Well, I may not have mentioned how much this last church job has netted us. We can afford it," he said.

Well, I just don't know what to say, except that I love you very much," she said.

"I know, Jan," Paul said softly, looking into her moist eyes.

Chapter 4

Early Summer

The car cruised along silently. They were well out of the city now. "It's like another world, isn't it? Our place in the country is so peaceful; I sometimes forget it's not that way everywhere," said Jan.

"But I enjoy plunging into the 'fast lane' for a short time, don't you, feeling the energy of that many people?" replied Paul. "And speaking of energy, isn't that Stephen Craig a 'feisty' one!"

"Oh, he is a doll," Jan said. "Jon and Sandi are such calm and caring parents. My! How they have grown up in the past year! So how does it feel to be a 'grandpa'?"

"I love it," he replied. "I think we may be making more frequent trips to Denver. Did you notice his tiny little hands? I had forgotten how small babies are," he reflected.

"I'm glad you were able to get away and go with me. I wasn't looking forward to seeing my father; but somehow I felt I had to, especially since I was going to be in the city to see my editor anyway. How did you feel after meeting my father?" she asked.

"I'll have to admit, Jan, that I was uncomfortable with Louis Tournier and can't really say why. I've thought about that several times and can't find a reason, except perhaps his 'condition.' He seems in very poor health, probably due to the alcoholism. Did he ask you if he could come and stay with us?"

"Yes, when you were not in the room. I had no reservations about telling him I felt he would have better care in the assisted living place. And, they will see that he stays 'on the wagon.' I think it is good that he mostly ran out of money or he would have drunk himself into an early grave, as they say. Not that it would have affected me. That sounds cruel, doesn't it? It's a very strange feeling to be drawn to someone you're afraid of and not know why you are afraid."

"I can't say that I understand it, Jan, but your feelings are your feelings. I had very wonderful parents and I sometimes wish you could have met them."

"Do you miss them?" she asked.

"Yes, in a way. But for a long time I've seen death as a natural transition, an essential rest, so to speak, that is vital to further evolving. To me, it fits into the universal rhythm of leaves falling, only to have new ones magically appear in the spring. Or consider the rests in music that gives more beauty to the notes, or night and day - I could go on and on - from the pulsing in and out of subatomic particles to the cycles of the stars."

"That's beautiful, Paul," Jan said. "Many cultures see the time between lives in a similar way. The Okinawans call it 'gusho.' The ancient Egyptians spoke of 'amenthe' where they dwelled in continual pleasure until deciding to take on a new body. Even the Hebrews spoke of 'pardish', the place from which they went out. Some now speak of it as a place of overwhelming illumination or being reabsorbed into the undifferentiated oneness or uninterrupted awareness. How's that for a 'mouthful'?"

"Those phrases are certainly more comforting to me than 'final judgment' or 'hellfire and brimstone forever,' but perhaps some feel they need that image to keep them on the 'straight and narrow,'" replied Paul.

"There is evidence that some early cultures, perhaps 20,000 years ago, believed that the life force was in the bones and that animals and people were reborn from their bones."

"That's an interesting theory," he said smiling.

"Since I heard about the therapy being done using past-life regression, I've done some reading on the subject and plan to do a lot more. It was one of the things I discussed with Mr. Mayer when I saw him. I may do an article," Jan said.

"Sounds very interesting," said Paul. "I understand the latest research in physics speaks of a cosmic pulse - sub atomic particles are constantly disappearing, turning into a wave or probability then reappearing or as we might say dying and being reborn."

"I am very interested in the way that quantum physics appears to be confirming what spiritual masters have said for centuries. That's part of what I must study. Several books have come out that explain newest discoveries in layman's terms, and that is good, because physics was not part of the required curriculum for English majors!" Jan said laughing. "But this area called 'metaphysics' really fascinates me."

"What exactly is metaphysics?" he asked.

"Well, this is not what the dictionary says, but to me it explores and attempts to explain all that we call supernatural, such things as clairvoyance, healing, channeling, and so-called miracles. Some say 'speculative philosophy' or perhaps that beyond the laws of physics. Do you know what Jesus said about these things?" she asked. Paul shook his head.

"'These things you shall do and more.'" she answered smiling. "Neat, huh?" They rode in silence for a while.

"Jan, do you think we gain anything if we don't have any conscious knowledge of what we are supposed to be working on this lifetime - no psychic flash of our grand mission?" he asked.

"Wow, that's a tough one," she replied. She thought a minute then went on, "Yes, I believe our inner self or soul, if you will, knows and gives us clues. We tend to go toward the things that bring us happiness; even the most unaware do that. Expressing our talent is one clue; you with your visions of beautiful buildings, me with writing and sharing things I see and learn. It seems the unconscious mind guides us or draws to us people and experiences that we need in order to see our path. A great mystery, but it seems absolutely accurate. When we know we have overcome a certain problem or learned a certain lesson, we seem to never encounter it again; we go on to other challenges." She paused, caught up in the beauty of the passing scenery. "How wonderful to get back into the mountains," she said softly. "It is so much easier to believe in the perfection of the universe here. I really did enjoy our afternoon at the Art Museum though. To me, artistic talent is truly a miracle."

"And artists probably think that the ability to express thoughts on paper is supernatural," he added, laughing.

"Did you know some people consider creativity a type of psychic phenomena?" She glanced briefly at him sideways and went on, "Yes, because they believe it flows from the sub or unconscious to the conscious mind. There are several fields of scientific research that are studying things that were considered foolish by most people only a few years ago. The medical field is studying the effect of negative ions on headache patients, for example. Are you familiar with ions?" she asked.

"Only vaguely from college chemistry classes," he replied.

"Well, oxygen molecules with a surplus of electrons have a negative charge. I think this makes them attach to other molecules more easily, which creates a positive field. I'm not sure; as I said physics was not my forte. But these negative ions are found in abundance in places like near waterfalls and they can be created. They seem to help recovery from burns and also allergy problems. Some people are very sensitive to these changes in the electrical field. A Russian researcher reported that changes in the hypothalamus might make one more sensitive to electromagnetic fields. Certain weather conditions can bring different electrical fields, such as the 'sharav' winds of the Sinai or the 'mistral' winds of France. There are excessive positive ions in these winds and cause many health problems as well as increases in accidents, crime rates and mental case admissions to the hospital."

"Well, let's not move to the Sinai then!" Paul said in mock seriousness, and then laughed.

"Oh, you!" Jan retorted. "But it is a fascinating area of study – the paranormal, altered states of consciousness and so on. In fact, a book written in the tenth century called *The Third Spiritual Alphabet* by Francisco de Osuna . . ."

"How do you remember all that?" he interrupted.

"Oh, I don't know; I think it stuck in my mind because it was the same as the city – I don't know why! I found it interesting" she retorted. "Anyway, the book told how to enter an altered state of consciousness by repeating a short self-composed prayer over and over for an hour in the morning and again in the evening."

"Wouldn't the Yaqui Indian way of mescaline or peyote be easier?" he interjected humorously.

Jan smiled. "Well, anyway, these are not new ideas. They are just being rediscovered or redistributed to other cultures; they're being explained in new ways to new groups of people. Einsteinian physicists and mystics are agreeing on several things: for one – the possibility of a unified field. To me, that is just another way of saying we need to consciously realize the underlying oneness of all things. Some say to find this state of mind is to discover the Tree of Life spoken of in Genesis" she paused. "What is that light?"

"What light, Jan?" he asked.

"I see colors. Oh, no!"

"What is it, darling?" Paul asked.

"It's the aura," she replied.

"Aura?"

"Migraine aura. Oh yes, it is starting now," said Jan.

"Oh, no. Shall I stop the car? Are your capsules in the overnight case?" he asked.

"No, they're here in my purse. Is there a bit of coffee left?" she asked.

He was already reaching for it. "Yes, I think so," he replied as she frantically searched her purse for the prescription bottle.

"Oh, I just hate this! Why now?" Jan said.

"Perhaps the increase in altitude," Paul offered weakly.

"I don't think so; we were at sea level in Cabo," she said wearily.

"Recline your seat, close your eyes and begin your affirmations or mantra," he suggested. They rode in silence for a while. He noticed she was near hyperventilation with the pain. "Breathe slowly, love, if you can. Any better?"

"No, worse. I'm getting nauseated," she replied.

"I will check the on-board navigation to see if there is an emergency room in the next town." He quickly pushed a few buttons and said, "It's only a few miles. Let me know if you need to stop."

He speeded up to somewhat over the speed limit. Soon a sign indicated that the medical center was just off the highway. He turned and quickly pulled up to the ER entrance.

"We're here, love. Lean on me," Paul offered as he opened her door and helped her out.

"Migraine," he said to the nurse who appeared at the emergency room door. She went into immediate action, helping Jan onto a gurney and grabbing a throw-up pan and lowering the lights in that section, seemingly all at the same time. "This is not her first migraine patient," thought Paul with relief as she disappeared momentarily to call the physician on duty.

"He's in the cafeteria; he will be right up," she assured them as she began 'vitals' and information.

Paul talked briefly with the physician when he appeared and gave the name of her prescription and when Jan had taken it. The calm doctor assured him that with an injection they would have her more comfortable in a short time. But after an hour Paul was becoming anxious, pacing back and forth.

Finally, the doctor came back in and said, "Your wife's blood pressure was almost dangerously high. That's the reason I'm keeping her under observation so long. I'd like to monitor her for awhile longer. I understand you are traveling through. Are you far from home?

"Only about an hour," Paul replied.

"Well, your wife should be able to finish the trip in a short while. Just wait here with her a little longer," the doctor said.

"Thank you," he said as the doctor hurried off to another room. "How's it going, lovely lady?" he asked softly, taking her hand.

"Oh, just tickety-boo," Jan replied weakly, smiling faintly.

"Well, we'll be tucking you in your bed at home in a short time."

"That sounds wonder . . ." her voice trailed off to nothing.

The nurse continued monitoring Jan's blood pressure from time to time.

⌒৲

Paul opened up the house quickly and came back to the garage. He lifted her out of the car and carried her up the steps. "This is like before," she mumbled.

"Yes, I carried you across the threshold on our wedding night," he replied.

"I had on . . . a white gown," she muttered.

"Darling, your gown was beige," he softly reminded.

"You put me by the fireplace . . . I almost died . . . Where is my habit?" she whispered.

He frowned as he laid her on the bed; it upset him not to be able to follow her thoughts. "Just rest, darling. Let me help you get your clothes off," he said as he slipped off her shoes and began unbuttoning her blouse. He couldn't seem to erase her last words about the habit from his mind as an image of a priest in a beige habit came to mind. "Priests usually wear black habits," he said to himself and tried to push it out of his mind.

⌒৲

As Paul came down the steps to the flagstone patio, he saw her perfect profile in the early morning sunshine that was flowing between the pines. Her absolute beauty tore at his heart, but more than that - her delicateness. He sensed a fragileness of emotions as well as body. Even with her loose, flowing tunic and pants of soft sage green, he suspected she had lost several pounds lately. "Good morning, my lovely lady," he said as he crossed the stone patio and sat in the teak patio chair beside her.

"Good morning, love," Jan said, smiling.

"You're out early. You're better," he stated.

"Yes, finally. It's about time, don't you think?" she replied.

"Well, it *has* been five days since our 'fun' trip from Denver," he responded.

"Yes, my lucky number," she said, somewhat lost in thought. "There is so much peace in this garden. It almost seems like a 'power spot' for me, if there is such a thing. Perhaps we create our own 'spots,'" she reflected softly.

"I can believe that," he replied. "I'm really glad you suggested the fountain and pool. The water lilies are doing great this year and have you noticed your herb bed? The rosemary and lavender are going wild," he said enthusiastically.

"Yes," she said looking at the plants with tenderness. "It's good that we have the gardener and automatic timer to water everything; I've been so out of it this past week. I'm sorry!" she said suddenly, turning to him with moist eyes. "I feel so worthless. I missed your open house yesterday. How did it go?" she asked.

"Oh, none of that. It was fine. At this point in my life, an open house is not a big deal. I'm just so glad to see you better and smiling," said Paul.

"I feel like I've lost those days. They are gone forever. My thoughts have been so full of hopelessness, as though an alien force is controlling my life, occasionally punishing me, just for the hell of it. What did I do to deserve this?" Her voice became lower reaching an intensely emotional whisper. "Am I going crazy?"

Paul calmly rose and knelt on one knee beside her and took her hand. "You are not crazy," he said firmly. "And no external power has any control over you. You are on the right track. Don't give up now. You told me that for several years now if there was anything you really wanted to know about, you were somewhat miraculously led to the person or book that could give you the answer. This is no different. 'Seek and you shall find,'" he quoted. "We've only begun to search."

"I'm tired, Paul. I'm tired of fighting. I talked to Dave; he is willing to work with me again but we both feel we've done about all we can along the lines of traditional therapy. He told me about a Dr. Morgan who has had good results working with past life regression. I suppose one would have to be open to that philosophy. He also mentioned a pain center in Scottsdale that is associated with a psychiatric center. I guess they claim to be having some rather remarkable results," Jan said in a flat tone without any enthusiasm. "They utilize biofeedback and body awareness and so on. I don't know. I don't want to be in a psychiatric ward. My friend, Peg, was committed once, several years ago when she slashed her wrists. She told me things you wouldn't believe that some of the patients did to the rooms in their anguish and craziness. It makes me shudder when I remember the scenes she described."

"Why are you talking about psychiatric care, Jan? There is nothing I can see that indicates that you are anywhere near that category."

"I don't know; just crazy thoughts, desperate feelings, and even weird nightmares. The pain gets to me, Paul. And the medication is worse. I see things."

"I'm so sorry." He paused. "Oh, that reminds me, Jan; when I was carrying you to the bedroom when we came home from Denver, you mentioned a habit. Do you remember that?" he asked.

"No, I have lots of bad habits," she said grinning impishly.

"No, no, clothing - like nuns and priests wear," he explained.

"Sweetie, everything from last week is a haze, a blur."

"Well, it doesn't matter. I was just curious. It seemed to stick in my mind," he assured her. "What do you think about a rose garden over there where we put pansies this year?"

"It sounds beautiful. But I've heard roses require quite a lot of care," she replied.

"Well, the gardener is very good and I may have a bit more time to be home in the upcoming months. I have turned two recent clients over to Keith. He seems to be coming along and is able to handle most things now. I'm still thinking of doing some traveling in Europe. Would you like that?"

Jan looked at him squarely and he noticed her seriousness as she said, "I cannot attempt anything like that until my 'problem' is better. I will not risk ruining something that important - and expensive. Can you see why I feel like an invalid, a burden?" she replied.

Paul rose from his chair again, kneeled in front of her, gently pulled her to him and held her very close. "You are definitely not a burden." He could feel her tears soaking through his shirt and felt so helpless in all this.

Chapter 5

Late Summer

At Jan's knock, a petite woman with silver white hair in a white terry lounge set appeared at the door. "Dr. Morgan?" Jan inquired.

"Yes. You're Jan. Come in dear," Clarice Morgan said warmly as she pushed open the door.

"Did Dave call you?" Jan asked.

"Yes, he did, Jan, and he explained what you are dealing with and briefly the progress you have made working with him," replied Dr. Morgan.

"Well, Dr. Morgan, there are times, like lately, when I feel I've made no progress at all," Jan said.

"Please, dear, call me Clarice. That is one reason I started to see people here at my home instead of the office. I do try to establish comfortableness before we begin - and I can dress comfy," she said smiling.

"I feel it already . . . uh, Clarice. Dave told me you had mostly given up your counseling practice, though you have had some remarkable results in the field of psychology," Jan said.

"Well . . . Dave has been a friend for many years and I consider *him* one of the best, so, let's sit in the sunroom," Clarice said as she led Jan through an immaculate house that gave the feeling of coziness. Entering the sunroom was like stepping into a room full of joy. It was mostly glass, partially shaded at this time of the afternoon by the house and the large oak trees in the green yard. Blooming plants hung at the windows and the white wicker furniture with fluffy floral cushions appeared to have grown there like the flowers. Jan realized she had just been standing there soaking up this beautiful environment. "I'm sorry, I was so captivated by this enchanting room," she stammered.

Clarice smiled. "Yes, there is a peace here. Please sit anywhere." She paused in thought a moment, then went on, "Jan, I assume, since you are here, that you know something about past life therapy and that you have some degree of acceptance of reincarnation."

"Yes, now it seems like I have always believed that, but actually I've only become aware of its implications in the past four or five years. Since Dave talked to me about your intuitive talents I've done some reading and find the subject fascinating, like something I've been searching for all my life. I'm planning to do more research and possibly write an article. Did Dave mention that I am a writer?"

"Yes, I knew that, Jan. Have you read Joel Whitten's book, or Morris Netherton's? Or, more recently, Michael Newton's?" Clarice asked.

"Only Dr. Netherton's," Jan replied.

"Then you know of the great number of people who have had dramatic healing of both physical and psychological disorders once they remember what happened in the past and understand why they are still carrying the event with them?" Jan shook her head in the affirmative, so Clarice continued, "A belief in an afterlife is older than history. More than 3000 years before Christ incarnated, the Sumerians killed the servants when the master died so that they might serve him in the next world. Plato spoke graphically of this period when one is not in the body form. The Egyptian Book of the Dead from around 1300 BC was originally titled, Going Forth in Light, which is much more positive-sounding, don't you think?"

Jan smiled and nodded, "It spoke of love as 'the everything,' much in the same way that Christ spoke of love."

"Yes!" said Clarice enthusiastically. "You have done your homework." She looked at Jan, beaming and Jan felt warmth radiate through her being.

"We cycle or pulse as the earth cycles, as the sun cycles, the plants rise from a seemingly dead piece of matter we call a seed, grow, change, fulfill their purpose, die and are reabsorbed into the earth, only to support the process again and again. We pulse with the universe because we are very much a part of it," Clarice emphasized. "Our eternal spirit never dies; we are an individu-alization of the Whole, the One Spirit. The Katha Upanishad of India, written in the 6th century BC said, 'The Self . . . does not die when the body dies. Concealed in the heart of all beings lies the *atma*, the Spirit, smaller than the smallest atom,' I am sure that is a translation word, 'and greater than the greatest spaces' . . ."

Clarice sat reflecting on the quote a moment. Then, bringing her attention back to Jan, said, "All the metaphysical research that has been done with countless numbers of people remembering their past, has shown us that the attitudes that we develop and the actions we take in one life will determine the challenges of the next life or lives to come. This is referred to as karma, but I think, that concept is misunderstood by many people. It is an attempt to put the vast universal principle of cause and effect into one word. It's an oversimplification, but it is a step toward bringing the idea to our 'western' awareness. We have to realize we are only beginning to understand our universe, our Selves, and our Creator, in terms of mass consciousness. As time goes, it was only a few days ago we believed the sun and stars revolved around the earth and that one could fall off the edge of the world!" Clarice laughed with Jan.

"So, we've come quite a distance in a few hundred years," she continued, "but we have far to go. Some things have not changed."

"In the Gnostic gospel, *Pistis Sophia*, we find the quote of Jesus, 'souls are poured from one into another of different bodies of the world.' In some of the North American Indian tribes, one who wanted to be a shaman had to recall his or her ten most recent deaths."

"Some, such as Edgar Cayce, who did their best to disprove rebirth, ended up being convinced of its truth. One psychologist would not give in until he had amassed a thousand cases saying the same thing. Of course, we have more than a billion people in Asia who believe it. Our Christian Bible in Galatians says, 'Whatsoever a man soweth . . .' which is very much like the quote from the Upanishad, 'As a man acts, so does he become . . . As a man's desire is, so is his destiny.' I'm rather intrigued by the last part of that quote. It indicates the power of our thoughts, our ability to create our 'destiny.' Gautama Buddha said, 'If you want to know the past, look at your present life. If you want to know the future, look at your present life.' So, that is what we want to look at - your present, your past," Clarice continued.

"Dr. Ian Stevenson is probably one of the most widely known investigators of reincarnation. Much of his work was with children in Thailand. He examined 200 birthmarks on children who claimed to have been killed in the previous life by an injury to that part of their body. He was able to verify 174 of these by medical documents that the person they claimed to have been, indeed, did die of an injury to that area. There have been many cases of children spontaneously recognizing older people still living that they knew in the previous life. This would indicate a rather short interim, in time as we think of it, between lives, though researchers have found this discarnate period can vary from months to hundreds of years. Of course, this area of research is very new; the picture is incomplete. Are you familiar with the work of Elizabeth Kübler-Ross?"

"I only know that she worked with and wrote about the terminally ill," Jan replied.

"Yes, she compiled a lot of observations about dying. It was her opinion that it is practically impossible to fulfill our entire destiny in one lifetime. I would add there is never an end to exploring Life. Talents and abilities are increased life after life."

"But, back to your pain, Jan. As I understand it, the medical world can find no definite physical cause, no brain tumor, or anything of that sort and Dave assures me he finds no psychological cause such as tension or repression. You seem to have a happy, well-balanced life, a fulfilling career and relationship. So, that leads us to the eternal spirit. Pain is not perceived by the inner self or spirit; it cannot know pain as the ego self or physical body does. Pain begins in the 'junction point' between body and soul. We come into each life with a purpose to grow or at least come another step closer to realizing how we 'fit' into the All. Pain or illness may be an impulse that rises from these deeper aspects of our Self, to prod us, so to speak, to understand our mission. We find in many people the pain turns up in a part of the body that is symbolically or directly connected to some karma, some need to understand, some facet of our self that is yet out of harmony or alignment with the Whole. Can you see how that can be, Jan?"

"Sort of," she replied. "I don't understand how much of this is provable. That is what I run up against, especially with my editor, in writing. Everyone wants scientific proof. Of course, if I can get relief from the headaches, I don't care if you do an incantation over a boiling pot of lizard lips!" Jan said laughing. Clarice laughed heartily with her.

"I'm very happy to see you have not lost your sense of humor about this," Clarice went on, "that is an important sign to me of your willingness to keep trying. One sort of proof that comes to mind is that of patients who have spoken and written down languages from the time they had regressed back into. Those extinct languages were corroborated by language experts to, indeed, be from the time the patient described. But I do not seek to prove anything, only to heal and learn. It was *Henri Poincaré* who said, 'It is by logic that we prove. It is by intuition that we discover.' I have found discovery and experience to be much more important to our evolution as persons and as a species; also much more satisfying and fun!"

"We go through several phases of development before we finally come to the path of conscious evolution, or deliberate creation as some say. One may follow this path with the help of one or all of many methods: meditation, transcendence, mysticism, religions, metaphysics and others; but whatever the method, it must include the wholehearted acceptance of the precept of love. Only by taking complete responsibility for all the things that happen to us can we evolve rapidly. As James Perkins said in his book, *Through Death to Rebirth*, 'To open the individual path inward is the most exalted of human endeavors . . .' So . . . the journey inward - remember that in this perfect universe made by an all-knowing Creator, there is complete safety."

She paused a moment to look into Jan's eyes to be sure she understood her emphasis. "Everything you need to know is within your self. Would a Creator who loves us unconditionally have it any other way - to leave us in the dark about things we need to know for our evolving? No, He/She would not."

"So, Jan, I think you might be more comfortable lying on the sofa," Clarice said as she fluffed several soft pillows under Jan's shoulders as she lay down, and she laid a soft cream and rose afghan on the back of the wicker couch. "Here is a coverlet if you should get cool. It sometimes happens. You will be focusing your energy so the body will be very quiescent while we explore. Her voice was taking on a soft monotone and Jan was already beginning to feel very relaxed. Clarice started a tape of soft music, something Jan had never heard before.

"Close your eyes and relax your entire being. There is nothing mystical or unusual about remembering your past. You can remember events of five years ago, you can remember events and feelings from your childhood, and you can remember events from your past before that. You are eternal," her voice intoned softly. "Jan, we want to go back to the time that is causing your pain in this lifetime. I am going to count down from five and with each number you will be more relaxed and start to progress back through your memories. You are in control at all times. You will observe the past like watching a movie. You'll not physically feel any of the pain you may remember. You are an observer and can come back to now at any time you choose . . . . Five . . . . You are very relaxed . . . . Four . . . . You want to remember the past . . . . Three . . . . You are still more relaxed in your mind and in your body . . . . Two . . . . You are coming into the memory area of the time that you want to see . . . . One . . . . You are now seeing yourself in this past life . . . . ." Clarice could see the movement of Jan's eyes under her eyelids as though she were dreaming. "Jan, would you like to tell me what you are seeing?" she asked very softly. The room was quiet; the music had ended.

"A church of brown stone . . . . It has a bell in a square tower," Jan whispered.

"Are you at the church?" Clarice asked.

"Yes, I am a nun . . ."

"Can you describe what you look like or remember your name?"

"I am Sister Janine of the Order of Poor Clares . . . I wear the soft beige homespun habit of the Franciscans."

"What are you doing, Sister Janine?"

"I am scrubbing the floors of the nave," Jan replied.

"Are there priests or other nuns?"

There was a long pause then Jan answered with surprise in her voice, "Sister Clare, you are there!"

"Yes, yes, I am seeing it myself now. Can you see the others?" Clarice asked softly.

"Yes . . . Sister Jacqueline, Father Paolo . . . . Father Paolo is so wonderful, so kind, caring, helpful . . ."

"Can you go forward now, Jan, to a time of significant experience or memory?" The silence was so long, Clarice said again, "Jan, you can go now to an event of importance, one you need to remember."

"I had to go to Lyon with Father Paolo because the Bishop ordered us to."

"Is that in France?"

"Yes . . . there is much unrest in the Holy Church about ones who have taken to the teachings of Martin Luther and John Calvin."

"You went to Lyon? Why?"

"The Bishop suspected Father Paolo of teaching heresy and he suspected us of . . . ."

"Yes, go on; it is alright to say whatever you feel or think."

"of . . uh. . . living as . . . husband and wife," Jan said softly.

"Are you?" asked Clarice.

"No, we are both serious, earnest about our vows of celibacy. But on the journey back, something happened."

"What happened, Janine?"

"The coachmen stop and take the horses down to the river for water. We are standing beside the roadway overlooking a beautiful valley . . . It seems to be spring, but a cold wind is blowing. I am shivering. Father Paolo wraps one side of his cape around me and pulls me to him. I surrender to the warmth of his body. I love him so much . . . He holds me tightly. I look into his eyes . . . . his clear blue eyes . . . our lips meet . . . we both realize our great love . . . It will not be the same now. Our love is too strong. Oh! The coachers are coming! I pull away from him. There is such a flood of feelings. I'm scared!"

"It's alright Jan. Do you want to go on to another event?"

"No, I'm scared!"

"Very well," Clarice said softly and calmly. "You are in control. I will count to three and you will be able to remember all the things you have seen. One . . . . Two . . . Three . . . ." After a minute, she said, "Do you feel ready to open your eyes?"

Jan slowly opened her eyes but remained lying down. She looked into Clarice's eyes. "You were there. You were Sister Clare."

"Yes, I began to see it also, Jan, Sister Janine. I felt something special when I met you at the door, but did not see it until you did. I had never gone into that lifetime before. You helped me remember."

"The names . . . our names, are similar . . . that's too weird," Jan said.

"No, not really. I've seen it before. Dr. Ian Stevenson reported that a common feature in many cases is an announcing dream in which the expectant mother has contact with the spirit of the coming child and a name is suggested to them."

"Father Paolo is my present husband; his name is Paul. I knew there must be some reason why we get along so well. His love is so pure," said Jan. "He looked different, but he's the same; I can tell. I don't know how; I just feel it. Perhaps, the blue eyes."

"Perhaps," said Clarice, "it is said, 'the eyes are the windows of the soul.' How do you feel?"

"I'm fine," said Jan, sitting up. "We didn't get there, did we?"

"There will be another day. It's best to approach gently. You were not ready today. I would like you to spend around an hour a day until our next meeting, meditating and quietly visualizing again the things you have seen today. Assimilate them thoroughly. This will help us to proceed."

"Alright, Clarice. Is there anything else I can do?"

"I think you already have an attitude of reverence and searching. Your motives are pure. Continue to affirm love for your self, and forgiveness of all."

"Yes, Clare . . . uh, Clarice. Thank you for helping me. I'm glad I found you," said Jan.

Clarice opened her arms and Jan hugged her tiny body feeling the warmth of her love. "You drive very carefully, dear. You are yet in a slight euphoria. I will see you . . . ah, next Tuesday at 2:00?" she asked glancing at her open appointment book. "Is that alright?"

"Yes, that's fine. Bye," said Jan as she hugged Clarice again and stepped out into a warm sunny afternoon. It was a shock - she was still in a cold, windy morning in France.

Chapter 6

Early Fall

The fire began to crackle and snap as Paul put more twigs in the fireplace. "It's amazing how a small fire can brighten a room and make it cozy. This primal sensation must have come from our cave people days," said Jan as she began making dinner at the other end of the little cabin.

"Fire is a miracle," he replied, absorbed almost to the point of hypnosis in his task. "Did you have a nice walk?"

"A wonderful walk! I hiked up the north trail to the top of the ledge and sat in the sun. You can see much of the mountain from there. It was *so* peaceful; I felt caught up in some kind of . . . 'trip,'" she struggled to describe the feeling. "It was like I would never want for anything again and as if I had the power to do anything. As Wordsworth said, *'with an eye made quiet by the power of harmony/ and the deep power of joy/ we see into the life of things.'* I'm so glad you arranged this *and* I want to thank you for the 'alone time.' I needed it."

"Well," he replied, "I sensed you did and I needed to repair that water valve for Don. They'll be closing up the cabin for the winter soon."

"Since the session with Dr. Morgan I've needed a lot of time to think."

"Why did you cancel your appointment with her, Jan?" asked Paul.

"I guess I felt scared. I can't quite put my finger on it. But after that 'whingdinger' of a migraine last week, I called her and we set a time for next Thursday," she replied.

"You said I was a priest at that time. How did you recognize that it was me?"

"I can't explain it. Just a recognition of your . . . uh, essence, perhaps? Do you know the 'feeling' you get when a person you know enters the room you are in? If you could not see you might still recognize their . . . 'presence.' That's the best I can explain it - recognition. Perhaps something about the eyes, your blue eyes."

"That's interesting, Jan. It always seemed to me I had known you before. I had just marked it up to what they call '*deja vu.*' You didn't recall why the kiss made you scared?"

"No, it was though a black curtain fell and everything vaporized," Jan replied.

"You're afraid to see what is behind that curtain?" he asked.

"It seems so." She busied herself with the soup in the silence intensified by the occasional pop of the fire. "Let's eat by the fireplace," she suggested. "Are there enough pillows there to sit on by the coffee table?"

"Sure," said Paul as he put all the pillows off the couch on the thick rug by the hearth. "The things you've told me have given me some questions about my interest in cathedrals and churches," he mused.

"And *my* interest in world religions and my acceptance of none of them," she added.

"Very interesting; I'm as excited about the next session as you are fearful. Do you think it would help if I went with you?"

"No, it's something I feel I must do alone," she replied as she brought the tray of fresh vegetables. "The cheese soup is almost ready." She sat down on the rug beside him. "This is just wonderful, Paul."

They sat silently watching the fire as the sun fell behind the ridge. "The aspens are starting to turn a little up high on the mountain. I'll bet it will be really pretty in two or three weeks."

"We'll take a drive then, perhaps to Telluride. O.K.?"

"Sure, I'll bring lots of film," Jan replied as she brought the steaming bowls of soup to the table. Paul got the basket of crackers. "I'll try to add to my 'Portraits of Fall' collection," she said.

"Work, work, work," he teased.

"No, fun, fun, fun," she countered laughing.

"Ummm, wonderful soup," said Paul. "This is almost too much for one man -the food, the fire, *and you!*" he said appreciatively.

Jan just smiled at him and was silent a minute, staring into the fire; then she said abruptly, "I would like my ashes scattered in one of these high mountain meadows."

"Paul's eyes met hers quickly. He stopped eating and gazed at her trying to comprehend this sudden change of mood. "Why are you talking about death?" he asked.

"I guess I've been thinking of death a lot in connection with this past life thing. It's obvious; if there *was* another life, there was a death and a period in between or perhaps several. Maybe that is what I don't want to remember - death. Intellectually, I believe death is not something to be feared. In fact, it seems it is something we could have a choice about. If we have free will in everything else why not in death? If we are fully aware, we should consciously know when we have finished our mission here. But, how many of us know what our mission is, or even that we have a mission?" She paused, thinking. "Death is just the other side of a coin called birth. Or as someone else said once, 'the death of Monday is the birth of Tuesday.' Just a point at which the consciousness 'decides,'" she gestured quotes in the air, "to experience another dimension - a rest that the spirit takes from the stimuli and contrast of the physical existence. There is no need for a physical focus, so it melts away - ashes to ashes - all part of the great overall scene of rest and activity, rest and activity," she paused, sipping her soup. "It just seems like there is so much peace in these mountains; I would like my dust to be a part of that peace, not that my soul would care. Well, so much for today's lecture on death!" Jan said laughing. "I hope I didn't depress you."

"Well, no, just sort of surprised me. It *is* a peaceful area; I like the idea of being scattered in a mountain meadow myself. Maybe I tend to be too logical, but I've had a couple of ideas about this running around in my head. We are told that some cosmic impulse or intent of the soul 'causes' us to manifest as focalized energy - a physical being. We choose to resume our development. Physics tells us that energy cannot be destroyed. So, my question is - when there is no longer a need for this manifestation and we become 'unmaterialized' - where is this energy? Is that what is meant by returning to the undifferentiated oneness? Or is the spirit a form of energy?" he questioned, staring into the fire.

"That gets way out there, doesn't it?" Jan agreed smiling. "The other thing that occurs to me about this energy is its vibrational rate. Each personality 'pulsates,' so to speak, at his or her particular speed. The rate of vibration of this energy is, to my thinking, determined by one's spiritual, mental and emotional states. In other words, a great master or teacher such as Jesus or Zoroaster, who spoke of recurring lives by the way, 'a highly evolved person,' one full of love for all, would have 'high vibes' as the slang phrase goes. Pure unconditional love supposedly creates the highest vibrational rate. So hate, fear, doubt would bring your rate down. The question is: if one reaches this high rate and maintains it or stabilizes it, does he or she become an ascended master? Is this what happened with Enoch of Old Testament fame? It records, 'And he was not; for God took him.'" Jan paused reflecting on the quote. "Did his body disappear? Were there ashes? Or - at what point or rate is one 'in' what is called unity consciousness or God consciousness? If vibes could be measured and each person put on the Grand Scale, where would I be? Or is it a competition?" she said laughing.

"Also, I've read that after death, the energy of the soul seeks its own vibrational level. Others of a similar rate would be at this same 'place,' if you will." Jan gestured quotation marks in the air with her hands. "This indicates to me that certain energy stays with the spirit and is not 'absorbed' into the All-That-Is, that it remains a portion or an 'entity.' So if you can imagine someone very filled with hate and fear when they die - would their vibes be so low they would sink to the level of two revolutions per century or 'r . . . p . . . c,'" she said *very* slowly, then laughed.

Turning serious again, she asked, "Is that what is referred to as 'hell'? I've always sort of rejected that concept, but perhaps that spirit would have so little 'energy' it would be miserable. You know how awful it feels to have no energy, as we sometimes say when we are ill. Would this soul not have enough 'umph' to reincarnate to work off its karma and just have to stay there or would it have to recuperate awhile?"

"So is it only in the physical form that we can effectively work on increasing our vibe rate?" Paul asked, placing more logs on the fire. "And, is that our purpose for being here? Or do we reincarnate until we are all at the 'acceptable' level and can harmoniously blend with the oneness, or God, if you will?"

"Interesting question," she replied smiling at him. They were silent for a bit. "Flames are so hypnotic," she said, staring at the leaping sparks.

"Yes," he replied, gazing at the beauty of her profile, highlighted by the soft firelight. "Would you let me try to sketch your portrait sometime this winter? Would you pose - be my model?" Paul asked softly.

She just smiled, never taking her eyes off the dancing flames. "I'll take that as a 'yes'," he said. The crackling fire was the only response.

"Have you ever heard the word, '*muga*,' as used by the Zen Buddhists?" she said slowly, nibbling on a cracker, scarcely coming out of her state of reverie.

"No, I don't think I have," he replied.

"It means 'experiencing here and now - being totally involved in the present moment.' That's how I feel now and I felt that up on the mountain today, sitting in the sunshine - oneness with everything. I can only describe it as blissful. Oh yes, I almost forgot - I wrote a poem for you up there. Can you reach my day pack there behind you?"

Paul twisted around for the pack and handed it to her. She dug inside, pulled out a small open notebook and handed it to him. Then she rose to carry the soup bowls to the sink.

Paul read:

Who Are You?

Have I known you before?
Your eyes know me
To the depths of my soul

Somehow, I know you
As I know myself.
We are as one.

In other places, other times,
We worked through all the problems.
Now there are none.

We have shared
The greatest love together:
To live and die as one.

Where do we go from here?
The universe is our playground
Forever.

His eyes were moist when she came back and sat beside him on the rug. "I don't even know what to say. That is so beautiful and expresses so much that I feel but have never told you," he said and put his arms around her and they melted together like the two parts of the yin/yang symbol flow together. Their bodies seemed to harmonize more fully than ever before, a choreography perfected. He pulled the blanket from the couch and spread it on the rug in front of the fireplace and arranged the pillows. She lay back, smiling at him. No words were needed. Her eyes never left his as he unbuttoned her sweater. The arousal she felt at his touch had never diminished. He knew exactly how to gently place his hands around her breasts and kiss her softly.

In Denver, Louis Tournier gasped for air, coughed and struggled to find the call button for the nurse. When she came into the room, she wondered if she should talk to the Doctor about alerting the next of kin about his deteriorating condition.

Chapter 7

Fall

The sunroom was transformed but no less enchanting. Jan noticed the floral cushions had been replaced with ones of warm rust and mahogany tones. The afternoon sun through the vibrantly colored leaves outside gave a bright, kaleidoscope effect.

"I'm always captivated by this room," Jan said. "It seems like nature surrounds and . . . infuses it." Clarice smiled.

"How have you been, Jan?" she asked.

"Somewhat better; a bad one two weeks ago prompted me to call again. I'm sorry I had to cancel last month," she replied.

"Don't be. Everything is perfect. It is best to do a thing when the time feels right. Effortless flow is the key. Bach spoke of this when asked how he found his melodies. He said, 'the problem is not tripping on them when I get out of bed in the morning,'" quoted Clarice as she started a tape of soft music. "Intuition is effortless. It's just there. The hardest part is removing the blinds from the windows, the roadblocks from the path. This effortlessness is part of the harmony of the universe; nothing is accomplished in struggle. Our inner self knows this - that there is never a need to suffer or fight. Happiness is our natural condition; joy expresses our harmony with the rest of the universe. And the universe continually sends us signals to guide us into alignment with it - in order to expand its perfection and harmony. Pain and discomfort is a clue that we are not in harmony. Our inner self picks up these signals and then transfers them to the junction; we spoke of this last time, the connecting point between the spiritual and the physical, where consciousness sprouts into matter."

"Yes," interjected Jan. "Paul and I were recently talking about that. It is still a huge mystery to me."

"Do you dance, Jan?" asked Clarice.

"Yes, I love to dance. It is how I keep in shape."

"Do you love music with a passion?" she asked.

"Of course; it touches me deeply," Jan replied with a questioning glance.

"I thought so. Then you've experienced the 'combustion of positive feelings.' Not just any sound can 'move' you. Buddha said, 'It is not in the body of the lute that one finds the true abode of music.' When one composes or creates - anything - the creation comes from the harmony of the universe through the spirit, out through the conscious mind and is put into manifestation. When we experience a work of art, a book, a song, we touch that manifesting again. When you are inspired, filled with enthusiasm or desire or love or are moved to compassion or gratitude, you have experienced the effortless flow from spiritual into physical. God takes joy in the smallest creative act of one of His offspring."

"That's beautiful, Clarice," said Jan. "You are so wise."

Clarice laughed, "I must agree with Socrates, who said, 'one knows nothing in comparison with what he should know.'" She laughed again. "The joy is in the learning. And we are learning. I'm amazed when I think of what Giordano Bruno wrote, 'God is glorified in countless suns, not in a single earth, but a thousand.' On February 19, 1600 he was tied to an iron stake and burned in the *Piazzo Camp dei Fiore* in Rome for that statement. Now we manufacture nerve gas as part of a defense program, so there is much yet for humankind to learn, but we are evolving. A new age is dawning. Aquarius will give us the opportunity to learn new lessons, gain new perspectives. This will be the age of personal freedom and individuality," Clarice said with fervor.

"I can see you do not believe we are going to destroy the Earth or blow it to 'smithereens,'" Jan said laughing.

"No, I don't. There may be some rather uncomfortable events, but I believe in the inherent perfection and harmony of the universe. Our consciousness - our collective or group consciousness as Jung called it - is becoming more global, more cosmic in nature, and that means many are becoming more aware of the order of the universe. This is our salvation, you might say, global as well as personal. On a personal level, this realization helps us to have the smoothest journey possible. The universal goal is the eventual evolution of all energy to the highest level. So, with seven billion people on this planet, it is imperative that we become conscious of our evolution.

99% of all the species that have lived on this Earth have died out. At first, this seems awful, a waste, but when you consider the perfection of the evolving Earth; it is beautiful. Darwin's ideas on natural selection have interesting implications especially since we've seen some changes in our environment lately. Timothy Ferris said, 'when environmental conditions change, the most exquisitely adapted individuals may find they no longer fit, then it is the freaks and the misfits who inherit the future.' And this, perhaps, may be applied spiritually or emotionally as well as physically, for in actuality all are one." Clarice paused, thinking. Jan stared at her in wonderment, thinking of all she might learn from this woman who seemed to be a storehouse of knowledge.

"I believe it was Seth," Clarice continued, "the entity that Jane Roberts channeled, that said, 'To change your world, you must change what you project.' To me this means one's thoughts. 'We form physical matter as effortlessly . . . as we breathe.' Note that word, 'effortless,' again; it pops up everywhere. Have you ever thought about the way our bodies form millions of cells every hour. This entity wanted us to know that we return again and again until we realize that our thoughts create our reality and that we must be responsible in our use of this creative energy. In other words, we must learn how to handle consciousness wisely.

"I think it was Kuhn who said, 'Revolutions and changes occur when there is an overall growing sense that an existing world-view has ceased to function adequately.' I believe that is what we are seeing in the Middle East now - evolving consciousness running up against some not so evolved. More people are becoming aware of universal harmony and order. Even in the sub-atomic world, everything tends to move toward order. We know that fear, anger, and hatred are 'out of order.' Pain is a manifestation of fear; some say fear is the withholding of love -- from our selves and our Source or the Oneness. But this manifestation in the form of illness or pain is 'good,' or perhaps I should say helpful, because it is a signal; the contrast is an aid to our understanding. From understanding comes awareness and from awareness, we evolve back into harmony or oneness. Quite a scenario, yes?"

"Yes, it is, Clarice. Almost beyond my scope!" said Jan.

"We speak of the aspects of spirit, mind and body as though they were separate entities. They are not, just different functions of the Whole. They are one within themselves and one with everything else. When fear and separation is gone - healing is spontaneous. Full realization of this oneness and perfection vaporizes the illusions of sin, sickness, old age, pain and death. Many believe full realization is the key to immortality, nirvana or enlightenment. Knowing that one is not the body, nor permanently attached to the body, but that one is linked eternally with the creative force of the universe is liberating."

"Along this same line," she continued, "of the power of our thoughts, in the early 1500s, in Switzerland, Paracelsus opposed the idea of separating the spirit from the healing process. He said, 'Man's physical body is formed from his invisible soul.' He believed people could be healed by their thoughts. Someone from one of the cancer centers was quoted as complaining, 'all major ills are being coped with by acupuncture, apricot pits, astrology or transcendental meditation!'" Clarice chuckled, "I should like to add past life regression to that list. I believe we incarnate so we can evolve our thought/spirit process and take it forward.

We choose our circumstances very carefully toward that end and continue to choreograph that process throughout our life. We come with an enthusiastic intent and to fulfill our intentions it helps if we become aware of this mission. Wholeness is the uniting of body, soul and conscious mind, or the unified field as some teachers say. Some call it the ground of being."

"There is a great deal of conjecture about this unified field," Clarice continued. "Quantum physics seems to be dancing all around it. The smallest particles, called quarks, fermions and, now, bosons, seem to have quite the little personalities, masquerading briefly as particles, just to toy with the scientists. Even Einstein was puzzled; he wrote to his friend Max Born, 'I find (it) quite intolerable that an electron exposed to radiation should choose of its own free will, not only its moment to jump off (orbit), but also its direction.' But this IS the case, just as with our own free will. I think we sometimes forget that our bodies are made of these smaller units of intelligence and that the quarks and electrons of Earth seem to be identical to and obey the same universal laws as those in the farthest galaxy. So perhaps oneness will be explained by science, who knows? I read that ten million trillion neutrinos travel harmlessly through our brain and bodies in a few seconds and in another few seconds are on the other side of the moon!" said Clarice incredulously.

"And scientists call metaphysics far out!" said Jan laughing. "I have heard that there is a mysterious conveyance of information within like species. I think the scientists call this the M field or morphogenetic field, more commonly known as the 'hundredth monkey' effect. I wonder if these speeding neutrinos are involved in this in any way."

"That's an interesting correlation, Jan," said Clarice. "Scientists say that some of the electrons in the nuclei of the atoms of your DNA cells joined together more than 5 billion years ago, before the Earth formed. That is quite a history one is carrying around, if that is so. Some feel the memory of our total experience, whether it is past or future, is carried in the DNA cells. It's easier for me to visualize an Akashic Record one can tap into than a cell particle that 'knows' the history of the universe. You see I have much to learn also. I do believe we are continuously tapped into Universal Mind, whatever that may be. Getting enough of the 'static' out of the way so we can recognize this connection is the assignment." The two smiled at each other.

"I have read that if one has a single-minded pursuit of truth and wholehearted practice of the highest principles she or he knows, one may 'bypass' some karma. Do you think that is true?" asked Jan.

"I really can't answer that, Jan," said the older woman. "There are ancient and modern scriptures to that effect. Jesus of Nazareth probably gave the best advice for overcoming karma when He said, `Love one another.' Love overcomes anything. But some feel that as long as there is the desire to do, to be or to possess, there will be karmic consequences. In his research, Dr. Joel Whitten found that the smoothest transition from this life to beyond death was accomplished by those who have spent their lives mold-ing the outer character with the soul's highest impulses. Our thoughts and actions do leave indelible impressions on the ethe-ric substance of the universe, whatever 'etheric' may be, and if these impressions are not in harmony with the perfection of the universe, they must at some point be balanced or brought to har-mony. It's an energy thing. That realization might encourage us to weigh each thought and deed carefully."

"I can see that," Jan agreed.

"The benefit, of course, is liberation," Clarice said. "So, rebirth grants us the means to learn from experience. That is why so many teachers are encouraging us to reprogram our subconscious with positive concepts like joy, peace and love. There are many now on Earth who have been raising their vibrational rate in this way. They may choose to be reborn just for the joy of this delicious experience, and in order to show others how to bring heaven onto earth. Another thought about your question on karma: many who have experienced life between lives regression have spoken of coming back with a plan. They also have stated that there is a lot of flexibility, depending on how quickly one realizes her karma. The script may be finished if we attain the ultimate goal of life: that is for the soul to know itself. How do we do that? I don't know; I'm not there," she said laughing.

"At the time of your past life that we are exploring," Clarice continued, "it was heresy to teach rebirth. The official edict across the Roman Empire had come in 553 AD. The Cathar heresy of the 13th century included a belief in reincarnation, which was savagely stamped out by the Inquisition. Plutarch, the Greek philosopher, wrote, 'Every soul . . . is ordained to wander between incarnations in the region between the moon and the Earth.' So, even our ideas about rebirth have evolved. But we are here to learn and I am ready to try to direct this journey if you are ready to travel," Clarice said, viewing Jan warmly.

"Yes, I think I am ready," Jan replied. She lay back on the couch and Clarice covered her with a Navajo patterned afghan, lit three candles on a tall stand at Jan's feet and said, "Jan, since your life was that of the Franciscan vows, I am going to begin with a quote of St. Francis. 'Oh Lord, make me an instrument of Thy peace, where there is hatred let me sow love, where there is darkness, light, and where there is sadness, joy.'" Her voice had taken on a soft monotone, and she continued, "Please close your eyes. We are going to count back from five again, Jan. You will become more and more relaxed. You are in control at all times. The mind is not bound by space or time. Your mind is free to be in any time, any place. You may experience being the observer and/ or the observed. The mind can simultaneously experience two or more streams of awareness. We need to tap into the stream that will take us to the past you need to experience consciously to be free. At five, we begin to be completely relaxed, the mind just floats easily, slowly going backward to childhood," Clarice intoned softly and paused for a minute . . . "Four . . . . you feel so relaxed the body seems to disappear." Clarice gave Jan time to fully absorb this. "Three . . . . you are totally relaxed and traveling

back, back through your memories . . . . relaxed . . . . relaxed . . . . .
Two . . . . It is very easy. . . . . You are now in France. You begin to
see that lifetime . . . . One . . . . . In this very relaxed state, you can
experience that time . . . . Can you tell me what you see?"

A child's voice came out of Jan's mouth, "*Mamá! Mamá!*" She
began to cry.

"Where are you, Janine?" Clarice asked softly.

"They are taking *mamá* away. They will not let me touch her.
They put a torch to our house; they say it is bad, that *mamá* had
a bad sickness. My aunt undresses me and throws the clothes on
the fire. She takes me wrapped in a blanket to her house, not far
away. The neighbors all stay away from us."

"Very good. Can you go on to another time, Janine?" intoned
Clarice.

Jan clutched her throat and coughed, gasping for air. "The
children are all out; they're all safe," she rasped between coughs.

"Where are you? What is happening?"

"The old part of the orphanage caught on fire. The smoke
awakened me. I got all the children in my charge down the stairs
safely. Such a huge blaze; it is so hot! But the children are gathered safely around me and I have the baby in my arms. Thank the
Lord." Jan said with a sigh of relief.

"Good, good," said Clarice. "Do you want to move forward
again?" Clarice waited patiently for she could see her patient was
traveling in time by the movement of the eyelids.

"Another fire . . . . a bonfire . . . *feu sacré la fete de noel* . . . the Holy
Fire of Noel . . . the villagers are all here for the blessing of the fire by
Father Paolo. A member of each family takes a stick from the holy
fire to light their hearth at home with its blessing. Some of the young
boys of eleven or twelve are honored to be the ones to carry the fire.
Oh, how I love these children, these people. It is so beautiful; light
snow on the ground, the warmth, the side of the Church illumined
by the flames . . . ." Jan's voice trailed off to silence. Only the soft tick-
ing of the clock by the door kept the room from seeming frozen in
time as the shadows lengthened in the late afternoon sun.

"Have you come to another scene, Janine?" Clarice asked very softly.

"The chapel was beautiful this morning at matins . . . the dawn coming . . . the candles flickering. Fall is in the air; I saw a *colchis* yesterday," Jan said slowly, savoring the memory, "winter is near. A few clouds are coming in now; it may rain today. My thoughts are mostly peaceful as I prepare the morning meal of cracked wheat. . . Thoughts of leaving here are a little disturbing. Paolo has made arrangements for me to go to the small convent that is supported by his mother's estate near Toulouse. He said he and his mother both know the sisters would take me in with love. He will come to Toulouse after Noel, after he helps the new friar get settled here. The trip to Rome will be postponed. My thoughts drift back to that day in summer when Paolo and I walked in the forest searching for mushrooms and talked and . . ." Jan's body jerked and she threw up her hands as though alarmed!

"What is happening, Janine," asked Clarice.

"A group of men with torches just rode onto the cloister. Oh, no! One has ridden into the chapel! Mother Marguerite is screaming . . ." Jan gasped again.

"What do you see, Janine. Tell me."

"A man bursts through the side door with a torch. I run out the back. If I can make it to the forest, maybe I will be safe! Where is Sister Mary? Perhaps she is in the grotto where I sent her for more wheat. Oh, no! A man on a horse is chasing me . . . I am nearly tripping on my habit. AAAGH!" Jan screamed.

"You are an observer, Jan; this is a memory, you cannot be hurt. Please go on," Clarice said softly.

Jan continued in a slightly calmer tone, but obviously caught in a great struggle, "He jumps off his horse and knocks me down; I can hardly breathe," she said gasping. "He is on top of me . . . NO!" her voice was rising in panic again. "He is ripping my habit, tearing my headpiece off. I can't understand his language; he is grabbing my breasts and grunting appreciatively. No!! No!! I can't get away. I hit at him . . . Oh!" Jan's head fell sideways on the pillow as though she had fainted.

"Jan, Jan," Clarice called out as she knelt beside the couch, "you are observing. What has happened?"

Jan roused, eyes still closed, and went on in a dazed voice, "He hit the side of my head with something; I can hardly see, the pain is so bad . . . . NO!!" she screamed again. "He is between my legs tearing at my habit and undergarments. 'No! I am with child.'"

Clarice looked at her with astonishment. "Go on, Janine; see it all the way through."

Jan was perspiring heavily. "As I look beyond the man, I see the church is burning. Oh, Paolo! He's coming. He's running; he has a staff in his hand. The man does not see him or hear him till he is almost upon him. NO!!" Jan screamed.

"The man swung around on his knees, and bringing out his sword, ran it through Paolo. Oh, Paolo," she cries. Then screams, 'You bastard, I hate you. I hate you! May God roast you in hell!' I am fighting him with every ounce of my strength. He is fighting me off with his free arm. 'I hate you!'" Jan screamed, her body shaking, hands clenched in rage.

Clarice broke in, "You are observing, Jan, like a movie. It is important to begin to forgive. Forgive, Janine."

"There is a shout up the hill; the man looks around. His companions are calling to him. He grunts in aggravation and grabs at his horse's reins."

"NO!! Please! The sword goes across the side of my neck. I hardly feel it, but I put my hand to my neck. The man jumped on his horse and galloped down the hill to join the others. Some of the men from the village are running up the hill toward the church. My neck is warm and as I look at my hand, I realize what has happened. I feel a movement in my abdomen and reach to touch the sign of life within me," Jan paused.

"There is a sound beside me. Paolo is pulling himself through the grass slowly toward me. Everything seems so dark, but isn't it morning? I reach out and Paolo reaches out; he grabs my hand.

Our hands lie together on the crushed *colchis* flowers that harkened the coming of winter. A peace begins to flow over me and it seems the light is coming through. My last thought is that our baby is dying with us . . . . . ."

The room was so silent; Jan was so still, it almost frightened Clarice. "Is that all that is necessary for you to see, Jan?" There was no response.

Clarice waited a moment, "Jan, this memory is finished. As I count from one to five you will journey back to present time. One . . . Two . . . Three . . . you are feeling more awake now . . . Four . . . Five . . . You can open your eyes now and you will remember all the things you have seen so that they can be an aid in your growth and evolution . . . . Jan?"

Jan was wet with perspiration, yet she was shivering slightly. Her hair around her face lay in soft damp little curls. Clarice was still kneeling beside her on the floor as Jan opened her eyes slowly and looked at her rather blankly. Then she smiled and said with relief, "I did it! I made it all the way!"

"You did wonderfully!" praised Clarice with tears in her eyes. "But it is only the first step, now you are ready to begin using what you have seen."

"What do you mean?" asked Jan.

"We want to stop the headaches and now we know from where they came, but the other step is to erase the karma by understanding *why* it came. Is the person who killed you, known to you in this life?" she asked.

Jan felt very sad and then she finally said, "Yes . . . he is my father."

"Well, that gives it a different aspect, doesn't it?" said Clarice. "The reaction is in the hate and fear that developed in those last few moments. The oversoul carries the memory of that impression or vibration that was left on the universal energy pattern. Bringing this to conscious awareness is a big step in balancing it, but the erasing is in forgiving. Forgive the man in France; forgive your father, forgive in your heart, forgive with sincerity. Your soul also carries all the beautiful qualities and talents accumulated in that lifetime and others that you can draw on and use to get past this bit of memory."

"Clarice, I feel like I've awakened from a dream, but is it Jan's dream or Janine's?"

Clarice just nodded her head in understanding. "Maybe the nightmares will cease now," Jan said. "Will Paul and I have to go through this again?"

"Karma is erased by understanding, forgiveness and love - mostly love," replied Clarice.

"You were burned to death in the church, weren't you . . . Sister Clare?" asked Jan.

"Yes, I was. I explored that lifetime on my own after our last session so I knew before we began part of what you would see. I did see that Sister Mary stayed in the grotto until the men had ridden away, then came up to try to save me, but I was almost gone already. I now understand my awe of fire better. Of course, I did not see the unborn child. How do you feel about that?"

"It seemed like there wasn't a lot of guilt, as one might expect there would be in such a situation. It seemed my love and that of Paolo was very pure. The child was not conceived out of lust. At least it feels that way. Yet, as the future plans indicated, the raising and sharing of the child would have been difficult and not in the traditions of the times. Was that why the death was drawn to us?"

"That is possible. There was also possibly some previous karma with the man known now as your father. How do you feel about him now?"

Jan sat up and stared out the windows at the falling oak leaves for a long time. "I can certainly see why I feared him and I believe I can let all the past go, and trust that all is perfect in God's universe." Jan's eyes met Clarice's as she nodded agreement.

"It seems that your father has reacted one way: alcoholism, to the karma that was incurred in that life and you reacted in another way," said Clarice. "Your pursuit of this and seeing it through is what I call conscious evolution. You have crossed one very big hurdle and there is no limit to what you may achieve now."

"*Reino de felicidad ultima*," Jan quoted softly, "the realm of ultimate happiness," she translated looking out the window again.

"As the Upanishads says, 'the self shines in space through knowing,' or as the Bible says, 'does one put a candle under a bushel?'" Clarice said smiling.

"That's a beautiful thought. Or as Peter Benchley said in *The Girl From the Sea of Cortez*, 'something missing found, an order imparted.' She was supported by the universe because she loved the balance of nature," said Jan.

"So, to go forward, we keep in mind the three qualities that the teacher from Nazareth gave the most importance to: faith, hope and charity. I've always been especially glad that hope was in there. We forget its great power at times," said Clarice.

"I'm still amazed at how I could see the scenes as from above and also be in them at the same time AND feel the emotions," said Jan.

"That's part of the oneness of all that we spoke of - the knower, the known and the knowing. We are capable of a great deal more than we are aware of. One of the theories added to the unified field theory in Einstein's time postulated that there are either 10 or 26 dimensions, others say eleven. Since we know only four dimensions - three of space and one of time - they conjectured that the other dimensions had collapsed into structures so tiny we do not notice them. We can, even while in this life, learn to utilize some of these other dimensions, and I believe we may have done that today."

Clarice paused. "The oneness of all is not a new idea. A belief in the unity of humankind with the cosmos was widespread among pre-literate peoples according to the evidence. Science tells us that the smallest unit of matter we can identify is most of the time more like a wave of potential energy, and it changes depending on how we choose to observe it. So, the nature of our observation influences the qualities it presents to us. Naturally, we relate this discovery to what we've been told by metaphysics: that thoughts, wishes, and desires are 'real things' and make an impression upon the universe. So, if the soul comes with unlimited power and potential and if thoughts are real and powerful things, you can see the vast potential that is untouched in every human being. That is why one must honor every other person, because in him or her is that spark of eternal vitality and power. As Christ said, 'Love thy neighbor as thyself.'"

"So we are each expressing Infinite Intelligence or Divine Mind in a unique way," added Jan.

"Yes, 'God within,' as the Quakers of the 17th century taught, which was also taught by the Valentinians of the 3rd century. Which brings healing to mind as being one of the powers we should certainly be capable of and some have had some success in it. But I believe with constant awareness of our thoughts and consciously affirming love and oneness, a great deal more could be done in healing and helping others."

"So, where do we go from here, Clare, uh, Clarice," said Jan catching her mistake.

Clarice smiled. "Is the anger and hatred that you felt mostly gone now, Jan?"

"Yes, mostly; I will need time to think and work on it, but I feel I have passed a 'hurdle,' as you said."

"I would like to work with you. I feel you have great insight and with your writing ability and connections, perhaps we can pass some help on to others."

"I would love that, Clarice!" said Jan as she tried to stand, but sank back down abruptly.

"Please, lie down again, Jan. You are too exhausted to drive. I didn't expect this. I will call your Paul and have him drive you home," said Clarice.

"But, my car . . ." Jan said weakly.

"I'll suggest he get a taxi or have an associate drive him over," she said as she stepped into the next room.

Fall

The breathing of Louis Tournier became easier. He felt a peace as never before. When the nurse checked on him, she observed closely for a few moments then took his wrist to check his pulse. "I've seen this before," she thought, "the peace before the end."

Chapter 8

Late Winter

Jan slipped out of her winter white coat and beret and was hanging them up as Paul came around the corner. "Ah, you're home," he said giving a long warm kiss.

"I just hate these late snow squalls; I'm so impatient for spring and so tired of wearing boots and coats! I'm ready to play tennis and go for a hike in the mountains," she exclaimed.

"Well, speaking of tennis, would you look at my plan for the guest house and tennis court? There is plenty of space for them beyond the rose garden, but would you prefer to have them run east-west or north-south?" asked Paul.

"Hmmm," Jan hummed looking at the layout he had spread on the bar. "Considering the prevailing winds, probably north-south, and I get the south court!" she said laughing, tickling him on the ribs.

Paul grabbed her and pulled her close. "It is so good to see you so vibrant. You have been like a 'whirling dervish' lately. How many articles have you sent in the past month?"

"Oh, several," she replied. "You can't imagine how wonderful it is not to live in the shadow of a migraine. That was like living inside a cocoon; did I ever show the poem I wrote about that last year?"

"No; I'd like to see it," he replied.

She brought a folder back from the study and handed him a page. Moistness came to his eyes as he read:

Cocoon

What is it like,
    Inside a cocoon?
Dark.
A tunnel,
But no light at the end.
Constricted and stuffy,
    Like a room
That needs to be aired out.
Muffled, isolated.
I can't hear my friends
    or loved ones clearly.
They seem far away,
Outside my barrier.
Nor can they hear
    my screams.
For I never know
When the dagger may enter
    the left wall.

The one who spun this prison
    is the only one
    who has the key.
And if I am inside,
How can I begin
    to peel away the outer layers?

Is it possible
That the butterfly
    will ever come out
    to fly again?

What is the name of this cocoon?

Migraine.

"Most people who don't have headaches do not realize the additional psychological stress that they inflict," Paul said shaking his head and looking at her sadly. "I'm so glad you're better; I can't believe the energy you've had lately."

"It's wonderful. You've been rather busy yourself, planning all this and the trip to the south of France, Spain and Italy. It's just six or seven weeks away now, isn't it?" Jan said.

"Yes. And we still have quite a lot to do: brush up on our French and get this project underway as soon as the snow goes away. It should be mostly finished by the time we return in late June. Keith will be directing the contractor while we are gone. It was helpful that Clarice could pinpoint the area of that lifetime more closely. Of course, we will go to Toulouse also."

"She is amazing," Jan said. "I just love working with her. We are planning a seminar for this summer and I am putting together the materials for it. She is truly an advanced soul. It's so energizing just to be with her."

"It seems like everything is moving so fast now. The guest house will be ready just in time for Jon and Sandi and little Craig, or I should say 'bruiser' Craig," he said laughing, "to visit in July. Then your Lynn will be here for the month of August. Do you think she will prefer the guest house or her usual room?"

"Oh, we can 'cross that bridge' when we get there. It really doesn't matter, everything will be ready. I'm just so excited about this trip abroad I can hardly wait. I wonder how it will feel to actually be there. They say the old *Villefranche* is very picturesque," she offered. "I checked online and believe the village I saw, from the things I remembered, to be *Villefranche de Rouergue*, not the *Villefranche* down by the Mediterranean nor the one north of Lyon."

"I'm especially interested in seeing many of the old churches and cathedrals. I hope this won't be boring for you," Paul inquired.

"Oh, of course not. I'll be 'snapping' away, from all angles!" Jan replied glancing out the window. "Oh, there comes the snow again! And I was thinking we could run over to La Casita for

185

dinner. Let's just build a fire in the fireplace, get out that nice bottle of Zinfandel you've been saving, some French bread and some gouda to soften by the fire."

"Great idea! Did I tell you that Dan wants to sell their cabin?"

"No. Could we . . . ?" she asked.

"Well, I thought about surprising you, but decided perhaps we should talk it over a bit. It does require some upkeep. That is why they are giving it up, since they are moving to Miami. Of course, they would be welcome to use it if they are back in Colorado."

"Of course! I think it's a wonderful idea," Jan replied as she brought the cheese and some fruit from the refrigerator. "Can we afford it?"

"Have you forgotten how much you put into savings from your recent 'flurry' of work?" he asked as he struck a match to the ready fireplace.

"Noooooo," she drawled. "It's been too much fun to call it work! Oh yes, I also want to add some autumn crocus to our flowerbeds as soon as spring gets here. I saw some in a catalog and they reminded me of something I saw in my regression. They are so gorgeous, especially the new hybrids." She had told him every detail of the regression that she could remember.

Paul drew the low table and some pillows in front of the fire that was beginning to crackle. "Sometimes this fireplace reminds me of what you told me about the life in France, when I carried you down from the cold cell to a bed by the fireplace. I wish I could see that scene for myself. Do you believe in soul mates, Jan?"

"Well, in light of recent remembrances, I would have to say 'yes. I don't know what 'forever' means, but I do believe we will have love for each other that long," Jan replied. The gaze between them seemed to fill the room.

Breaking the spell of their eyes, Jan continued, "You probably will remember in time; you are open to it. You seem to have more thoughts about the spirit side of life, or at least talk about it more than you used to. Will we have another lifetime together?" She wondered out loud.

"Well, I hope so. The amazing results of your regression have given me a lot to ponder, and has opened some closed doors inside me. I find it interesting that we were Franciscans in that life and now the new Pope has chosen the name of Francis and seems to emulate him."

"I'm glad my 'journey' has opened some doors for you too. Would you open this wine bottle?" she asked, as she placed long stemmed wine glasses on the low table by the fire.

"Ah, the special cut glass. What is the occasion?"

"The occasion is that I love you and I am very happy," she replied.

"Ditto, ditto!" Paul exclaimed, leaning over and giving her a long kiss. "Do you suppose the 'nun' would allow the 'priest' to carry her *up* the stairs to the bedroom after dinner? He has some very carnal ideas in his mind."

Jan giggled and stuffed a chunk of French bread in his mouth. The fire crackled on.

Made in the USA
Charleston, SC
24 February 2014